Before the R

The Gypsy's Curse

By Soraya

To Amy,

Blessings

Soraya

ISBN: 1517711819

ISBN-13: 9781517711818

Part 1 Coralina's Story

Chapter 1

February 1873

Coralina Kelly sat on the padded bench beside the thick brown woollen curtain that closed off the sleeping area in the wagon, and she listened to her mother's feeble cries. She was sitting on her hands, because she knew that if she didn't keep them under her legs, she would have bitten her nails down until they bled. She rocked backwards and forward in her space; she was scared. She was the only child to have survived birthing, all the others had come away before their time, and she could remember when two boys had been born, but they were blue when they came out. She hadn't seen them but she had heard the aunties talking. They would have been her brothers, and she was sad that they hadn't lived. She was sad for her Mam too, because she cried whenever anyone in the camp birthed a new baby.

"Push, push, try harder lass," she heard old Mither Morrison saying.

The men were outside leaving the women to look after things, and she was alone in the wagon, separated from the others only by the curtain. She wanted to pee so badly, but she was afraid to leave, not that she was any help, but still, she didn't want to run through the dark to the toilet tent to relieve herself of her full bladder, just in case she was needed. Finally, when she could hold it no longer, she left the wagon at a run.

"Where ye goin' lass?" her father John called as she scooted past him. He and the others were sitting around the campfire patiently, if worriedly, waiting for the birth of the next child, sharing a bottle of whisky, and silently praying that all would be well.

"Ah'm goin' tae the dunny Da."

"Straight back Coralina, mind now, straight back."

The Gypsies' camp was set in a clearing surrounded by trees near Glasgow Green and close to the River Clyde. There was a narrow road close by, but no one could see the camp from there, and that was fine because their privacy was important. Eight wagons were on this camp, nearly forty Gypsies in all, and they were relatives of each other by birth, marriage, or close kinship. This location gave them access to all the places that they would travel to, selling their wares or services, whether they were heading to the Ayrshire coast or to villages and towns further afield. The wagons were in a semi circle, with a campfire in the middle. Over the fire stood a Chitty Prop, a three legged cast iron frame for suspending a large kettle for boiling water. At meal times, the kettle would be replaced with a heavy iron pot for cooking soups and stews.

Off she ran to the space that had been prepared, which contained a large galvanised steel bin. A lid with a hole in the centre, forming a seat, had been fashioned out of wood so that anyone who needed to use it could sit without touching the cold hard steel. A canvas hap was fastened to the wooden frame of the dunny and gave some privacy when it was in use. Coralina hitched up her thick woollen skirt and dragged at her knickers, pulling them down as far as her thighs, and then she squatted over the seat. She sighed with relief as she emptied her bladder; she had held it in for so long that she thought she would never stop. She paused when she had finished, hoping the last drips had fallen before she hitched up her knickers, and hurried back to the wagon.

She could smell the wood smoke from the fire and as she came through the trees, the light from the fire guided her. She could see the shadows of the men sitting around the fire, wearing their thick jackets, caps, and scarves to keep themselves warm in the cold February air. She could hear their whispered conversations but couldn't make out what they were saying. The heat from the fire warmed her face as she ran past it, and quietly crept back into the wagon. She was shivering now, and grabbing a blanket, she threw it over her shoulders. Once more, she took her place on the bench in the sitting area. She didn't know what time it was but she knew that it had been hours and hours. It would be morning soon and still she sat.

Mither Morrison had been in and out several times demanding more hot water as she tried to help Mary Ellen, her daughter-in-law, deliver her baby. Coralina didn't know what all the hot water was for, but Mither Morrison needed plenty of it. Just as the day was breaking she heard a funny little noise, a squeak almost, and then loud lusty cries. She knew, as her heart filled with joy and excitement, that the baby had come and it wasn't blue, she didn't think blue babies cried. She was excited and happy to have a new baby brother or sister, but as she listened, she realised that it had all gone very quiet, apart from the little noises the new baby was making.

Still she listened, and then Mither Morrison came out. At fifty-three, she was the oldest mother in their camp, and the 'Mither' in any camp was always shown the utmost respect and always had the best of things, partly because some of the residents would be her grown children, and partly because everyone in any camp made sure that the Mither had everything that she needed. She had been quite a character in her day, and even yet, as old as she was, for in those days being in your fifties was a good age, she still managed to bring a spark of light during heavy or hard times. She could make everyone laugh with the old stories she told, and when the occasion warranted it, she could dance a jig with the best of them, though her arthritic bones meant that her jig didn't last very long. With a word or a look, the Mither could make a man feel ten feet tall or chastise him and reduce him to feeling that he was ten years old. She was held in such esteem that she seldom had to chastise, and was more likely to nod and say, "Well done lad, aye well done," and the lad in question, though twenty-four or forty would puff up his chest proudly.

Mither Morrison's hair, once red, was now as white as snow. She wore it partly covered by a colourful thick woollen chequered scarf that she had wrapped around the length of her hair at the back of her neck, and twisted and tied to one side. Her hair had receded back from her forehead a little, exposing a deep brow over watery eyes once as blue as the sky on a summers day. Though her skin was pale, her cheeks were rosy red from daily exposure to the fresh air and the elements. A thick brown woollen dress came down to her ankles, and over it was a sleeveless v-neck jumper hand knitted using many different colours of wool. Over one shoulder was a woollen blanket of reds, yellows, and blues, and the toes of chunky black boots peeped out from her ensemble. She wore heavy gold hoops in her ears and fine gold bangles dangled on her thin wrists as she moved. Her jewellery, and the bright colours that she wore, always drew attention wherever she went.

She was proud of her family too, her son George was married to Mary Ellen's sister Isabella, and they had given her three fine granddaughters. The last one, a late baby, was little Daisy, not yet weaned onto solids, Nellie was five and Jennie was ten. Isabella had miscarried more than once, so she cherished her girls and she was a good mother.

Chapter 2

Coralina looked up as Mither Morrison came through the thick dividing curtain. She realised that the Mither was carrying the tiny baby wrapped in the new white shawl that her mother had knitted. The Mither handed the baby to Coralina.

"Here, watch whit yer daein', an' take the bairn tae yer Auntie Isabella, she'll see tae her. It's a wee lassie."

Coralina looked at the Mither and wondered why she had tears on her face. This was a happy time she thought, as she tenderly and carefully took the new baby in her arms. This tiny baby was her little sister and she was overjoyed. She looked back at the Mither and then suddenly felt confused. She wondered why she had to take the bairn to her Auntie Isabella. Coralina had a worried expression, her eyes were wide and her mouth gaped in surprise, but the Mither only said, "Tell yer Da tae come in on yer way oot."

Coralina stepped into the doorway pausing above the wooden steps, and then made her way slowly down with the baby in her arms. All the men stood suddenly and stared at her. They looked at her anxiously first, and then, as one, they looked at her father as he yelled, "Mary Ellen, nooooo, nooooo!" He screamed for his wife. He groaned as though in agony, as he realised that this could only mean one thing. Coralina, frightened by this sudden change, watched as the men grabbed her father, and held him as he cried. She skirted around them and ran over to her Auntie Isabella's.

Isabella, as well as everyone else in the camp, had been waiting and watching from her wagon as her sister struggled in the throes of childbirth.

"Come in hinny, I'll take the bairn. Go and sit down." Isabella did her best to hide her grief as she took the baby in her arms. Coralina climbed the steps and followed her aunt into her wagon, sat on the bench and watched as Isabella opened her top and fastened her little sister to her ample breast.

"She needs feedin," she said by way of an explanation.

"How come you're feedin her?"

"I'm sorry lass, ye'll have tae wait till the Mither speaks tae ye."

Coralina stood up to go back to her wagon. She was confused and frightened, and wanted to know why her aunt was feeding her baby sister and not her mother. She wanted to know what was wrong with her father.

"Sit doon lass, stay where ye are, Mither will come for ye when its time."

Coralina was staring at her aunt and she could see that she was upset. Tears began to run down Coralina's face. She didn't know what or why but she knew that something was wrong. She watched her little sister suckle, and she watched as Isabella moved her from one breast to the other. When she was finished feeding, and the baby was content and sleeping, Isabella reached over and placed the baby in Coralina's arms.

"She'll be yours to look after noo Coralina."

Not quite understanding the full implication of the words that her aunt had spoken, Coralina held the baby close, inhaling that new baby smell, and gazed into the child's sleeping face. She was overwhelmed with a love that she hadn't known existed.

"I'm yer big sister," she whispered, and she kissed the baby on her soft cheek.

"Ah'll aye look after ye," she said, as she rocked back and forward lulling the new baby.

A short while later, Mither Morrison came into Isabella's wagon, and the two women, the younger and the older, looked solemnly at each other as the Mither sat beside Coralina.

"Whit age are ye now hinny?" she asked, although she knew the answer to that question.

"Ah'm seven Mither, Ah'm nearly eight, Ah won't drop her or onythin', Ah'll be careful Mither."

"I, Ah ken ye will lass, Ah ken ye will, yer young yet but yer gonnae have to be strong for Ah have summat tae tell ye."

"Is it ma Da?"

"No hinny it's no' yer Da, it's yer Mam. She didnae make it. She gave her last breath tae yer wee sister."

"Whit dae ye mean Mither."

"She's gone lass, she's gone tae heaven tae be wi' the angels, an' ye'll have tae look after wee Mary here. She's your responsibility noo. Gie her tae me an' away ye go across an' say yer farewell tae yer Mam."

Coralina's eyes were wide with terror as she thought about what the Mither was saying. She let her take baby Mary in her arms and in a flash, she was out of the wagon, jumping down the steps, and there, amidst the wagons, was a trestle surrounded by other members of the camp, some were family, and some were friends. As she approached, they parted and she could see her mother lying on the trestle. Thick green glass jars containing lit candles were set around the trestle, but there was space enough for her to approach closely.

"Mam, Mam," she cried as she ran over.

She knew the custom for laying out the dead; she had seen it before and she realised that her mother was gone. She reached over and stroked her mother's cold face, the face that she loved so much, and then she touched her mother's hands, folded over her chest. She stroked her mother's raven hair and she tried to reach up to kiss her, but she was too small. She suddenly felt strong hands lift her up, she knew those hands; they were her father's hands.

"Be strong lass," he whispered to her as he her high enough to reach her mother's lips.

As he put her down, she turned, leapt into his arms once more, and sobbed into his strong chest. Tears coursed down John Kelly's face as he held his sobbing daughter in his arms. He could hear the quiet sobs of those who grieved with him.

The days following her mother's funeral were a blur to Coralina. Her grief was such that she gave all her attention to her baby sister, and the only time that she was parted from her was when her aunt put Mary to her breast.

"Does that make you Mary's Mam now that yer feedin' her?" she asked one day.

Her aunt looked up and smiled kindly, for she was glad that Coralina had spoken at all.

"No lass, Ah'll no' be her Mam, but Ah'll aye love her as though she was ma ain. She's takin' ma milk so there will aye be a part o' me in her."

"Ah love ye tae Auntie Isabella, and Ah'm glad ye had spare milk."

Isabella smiled, "A mithers' body's a miracle for it gives as much milk as is needed, even if Ah had two suckling bairns Ah could still feed a third. Ah'm still makin' milk for yer wee cousin Daisy, an' ma body'll make as much as Ah need."

Coralina gazed at her aunt with admiration and love in her young eyes. She thought that she was beautiful with her smooth skin and her long straight brown hair cascading over one shoulder. Isabella looked down into Mary's contented face as she fed her. Coralina thought that she looked like an angel, though she had never seen an angel, she was sure that if she had it would look just like her aunt. Thinking of angels made Coralina think of her Mam, and suddenly, the tears began to fall, and they wouldn't stop. Soon she was sobbing; she cried and sobbed, and cried and sobbed some more. She wasn't aware of Mither Morrison coming in, nor was she aware of her father picking her up. He carried her across to the Mithers wagon where they were staying temporarily, put her down on her bed, and covered her with a thick blanket. He sat with her stroking her hair, and he cried silent tears as he wished that things could have been different for his two girls. He knew the road ahead would be a hard one, but he promised himself that he would do his very best by his daughters. Finally, when Coralina was in a deep sleep he rose and left her to rest.

Much later, Coralina woke up her father sat on the edge of her bed.

"Sit up an' take some soup hinny."

She didn't know why but for some reason she felt much lighter. She sat up and her father spoon-fed her from the thick earthenware bowl. Each time he put the spoon to her mouth she would raise her eyes, and look into his strong handsome face. He looked older and sad, and she wondered if she was sick and maybe she was going to go to heaven to be with the angels too.

"Ah'm Ah sick Da?" she asked between spoonfuls.

"No lass, yer no' sick, yer just sad, dae ye feel sick?"

"No Da, Ah feel good."

"Here, take the bowl an' finish yer soup, and then go ower an' help yer Auntie Isabella wi' yer wee sister." He handed her the bowl and stood up to leave the wagon and then he turned and looked down at her, "Yer a good lass hinny, and yer Mam would be proud o' ye. Ah'll be away for a few days hinny so ye'll bide here wi' Mither Morrison until Ah come back."

Chapter 3

John and other members of the camp had held a wake for Mary Ellen until it was time for her burial at Janefield Cemetery. Now that the funeral was over, as was the custom, John and some of the other men in the camp would take the wagon away and burn it. It was thought to be bad luck to live in a wagon in which someone had died. Those who could not afford to replace their home would sell it to a dealer and a new one purchased. The wagon with all the deceased person's possessions was burnt, but there was one thing that John wouldn't burn. Mary Ellen had often spoken to him about the pretty dress she had worn when they had married. She had wrapped it carefully in brown paper and put it away for safekeeping. Each year she took it out, aired it, and treasured the memories it evoked. She always said that one day a daughter might wear the dress on her wedding day.

John took the brown paper parcel across to Isabella's wagon, "Ah've a favour tae ask ye? Ah've Mary Ellen's weddin' dress here. She aye said that someday her lassie might wear it an' Ah cannae bear to burn it. Whit dae ye think. Dae ye think Ah should keep it?"

"Aye John, Ah think ye should 'cause it was her wish, gie it here an' Ah'll take care o' it."

Wagon's were always eye catching and beautifully decorated with the woodwork intricately carved, decorated with fancy scrollwork, and painted in bright colours. More often than not, they would be in a bow-topped style with a heavy canvas cover. John rode to a dealer in the Borders and he had found a wagon, built entirely of wood. It had a narrow floor with the sides sloping out and upwards towards a curved wooden roof. The trimmings were carved in fancy patterns and painted red and gold. Two small spoke wheels to the front and two large spoke wheels to the back attached to the undercarriage giving the frame a good strong foundation. The inside contained everything needed for a family. There was a narrow bed suspended from the roof, which gave access below it to the front of the wagon where Coralina could climb through the stable style doorway to sit by him as he led his horses during their travels. A wood burning 'Queenie' stove fitted against one side would keep them warm during the cold winters, and the flat plate on top of the stove would keep water hot in a small kettle. A bench seat fixed to the opposite wall gave them a place to sit, watch the flames, and chat about their day. There was a plump cushion covered in a fancy tapestry on the bench which when lifted out, revealed a hinged strip of wood that could be unfolded creating a bed, which was perfect for Coralina, and as Mary grew both girls would be able to share it. Tucked away to one side there was a folding table, with two stools in front of it. There was plenty of storage room below the wagon, and between the wheels, and John knew that he could store his small cart, and many other possessions there. Gypsies always enjoyed cooking their food outside on an open fire so there was no need for anything else in the wagon and he was sure that Coralina would be pleased and surprised with their new home.

John was away for more than a week and during that time Coralina watched for her father's return. Isabella and Mither Morrison gave her lots of attention and love but she was understandably very sad.

Grief takes its time to pass and everyone grieves in their own way. Some find solace in tears and solitude, others find it in anger or in work, but Coralina found her solace in looking after little Mary. Sometimes when she looked at Mary, she could see a likeness to her mother and that too gave her comfort. She talked to Mary all the time, and Mary's gaze seldom left

Coralina's face. Gradually, day by day, Coralina recovered from the trauma and sadness of losing the mother that she had loved so much.

Coralina heard the commotion before she saw what it was about and when she went to investigate, she saw a beautiful red and gold wagon approaching. Her father was at the reins leading two horses, which he had purchased with the wagon, and his own horse tethered on a rope behind the wagon. Everyone had come out to see and admire John's purchase. Coralina had missed her father; she was excited by his return, but even more excited by the new wagon. Before long the horses were unhitched and led off to graze in a space adjacent to John's other horses giving them time to get to know each other before they would graze together.

Coralina climbed into their new home and sat on the bench opposite the stove. Her eyes were wide as she drew her hands over the tapestry seating and surveyed her new surroundings. One by one, other's came to call and give their best wishes for luck in their new home and each of them brought something useful for them to use. Linens for their beds, Tilly lamps to light their home on dark nights, pots pans or dishes and John was grateful for the support that he had received.

The weather was improving, summer was coming, and Coralina spent her days tidying the wagon, though there wasn't much to tidy, and learning from her aunt how to look after baby Mary. Mentoring Coralina helped Isabella to take her mind off losing her sister. She was a patient teacher, and delighted in showing Coralina how to break Mary's wind after her feed and how to change her. She taught Coralina how to clean the soiled nappies and care for Mary's clothes. Coralina already knew how to care for things around the wagon because she had often helped her mother. Many of the things that she had helped with had become her responsibility now, but she didn't disappoint anyone, and merely took these things in her stride.

When Mary wasn't being fed, Coralina would hold her to her chest and then wrap a big shawl around her shoulders. She then wrapped the ends of the shawl around her tiny waist, crossing them over each other and tying them at the front underneath Mary to support her. For the first three months of Mary's life, Coralina carried her like that everywhere she went. Mary grew fast with the love and care provided for her. As she grew heavier, Coralina began to carry her, still wrapped in the big shawl, but piggyback fashion, and baby Mary's big brown eyes took in every detail over Coralina's shoulders wherever Coralina went.

Chapter 4

George Morrison, Isabella's husband, had inherited his smithing skills from his late father, but smithing wasn't his only skill and he enjoyed working with scraps of wood that he came across. He often saw Coralina struggling with Mary on her back, and with that in mind, he began to put together a cart out of an old wooden box. Gypsies wouldn't discard anything that could be used again, and often found uses for things that home dwellers discarded. He added four small wheels to the box, fashioned a wooden handle, and then lined the box with a pillow stuffed with old clean rags that Isabella had washed and dried for him. He presented the cart to Coralina one day when Mary was about three months old. Coralina saw her Uncle George approaching with the cart. He had to stoop to push it because he had designed it so that it would fit Coralina's height. She watched him and wondered.

"Whit's that ye have there Uncle George?"

"Ye've been carryin' Mary aboot a while hinny, she must be getting heavy. Ah've made this so that ye can shove her instead."

"Uncle George! Ye didnae, did ye, is it really for wee Mary?"

There were tears in his eyes as he looked at Coralina's excited face. He smiled proudly at her.

"Here, gie me the bairn, let's see if she likes it."

Carefully he took Mary from her arms and placed her in the little cart. "She likes it," laughed Coralina as she looked at Mary who was kicking her heels on the soft pillow below her.

"Aye hinny, Ah think she does."

"Whit's that ye have there George," laughed one of the women, "Ah could be daein' wi' wan o' them."

Coralina could prop Mary up or lay her down, and for a while, she amused herself and Mary by just practising these things, and by pushing her around the camp to show the aunties' Mary's new cart. On fine days, she would leave Mary sitting in the cart in the fresh summer air outside the wagon. At night, when chores were done and Mary was settled, Coralina would climb into her bed in the wagon and watch over Mary in her crib before she herself would drift into sleep, listening to the quiet chatter of the adults who were sitting around the campfire. Many of the adults preferred to sleep outside, especially those with bigger families. In fine weather, they would sleep under the stars but in foul weather, they would erect a bender, then dismantle it and stow it away in the morning. The bender was easily constructed using cut saplings that they carried with them stored under the wagon, or replaced fresh if required, and these were stuck into the ground and covered with a canvas

Each morning after changing Mary's dirty nappy, Coralina would carry her to her aunt to be fed, and then she would run back to her wagon collecting hot water from the kettle to wipe surfaces and wash cups and plates. When all her tasks were done, Coralina would take Mary's dirty nappies and drop the soils in into the dunny before leaving them to soak in a tin pail. Later Isabella would boil them in the large tinny set aside for the wives to boil their whites. Travelling women always wanted to have the whitest wash, and Heaven help those who hung out a white wash with stains showing; they were a very particular lot.

Coralina's mother had taught her to wash her hands and face every morning, and once a week, her father would be bring out the big tin bath from under the wagon, and fill it with warm water to bathe in. Coralina loved sitting in the bath and now that she had Mary to look after, her father would hand the baby into the tinny, and Coralina would bathe and play with Mary while her father would look on proudly as his children laughed.

"Come on now," he would say, "gie me the bairn and get yer self scrubbed, dried, and dressed."

While John dried and dressed Mary, he would think sadly about Mary Ellen. Each time he looked at his children, he saw their resemblance to their mother. When she was finished, Coralina would reach for the towel and climb out of the bath.

"That's it, into bed and face the wall," he would say, before stripping down and climbing into the tinny for an all over scrub.

Every day when chores were done, the girls in the camp would go and sit with Mither Morrison to listen to her stories. She taught the girls how to sew, knit, and crochet. She taught them how to unpick a knitted jumper and to rewind the wool so that it could be used several times. Arthritis prevented the Mither from doing many of these things with her own hands but it did not stop her from teaching the youngsters. Whilst the younger ones practiced their skills, the old Mither would talk to them, teach them about their history, and sing songs of old.

Coralina loved taking Mary across the camp to sit with the Mither. In the spring, summer, and autumn, the girls would walk in the woods and fields with her gathering wild herbs and flowers, and as they walked, she spoke to them, telling them the best way to dry herbs for use in the winter when the land rested and when things were scarce. She spoke to them about the medicinal uses of different leaves or roots that would make a tea or a poultice to treat wounds, boils, or stomach pains. Those who heard her words did not realise that they were learning valuable survival skills, but these words were remembered, and passed on. Often while the women went about their business, the children's voices were heard through the trees as they learned the words of their songs. The Mither would recite the words and the children would repeat them, sometimes laughing as they did so.

Nettle stings when ye gang past

But grab it noo an' grab it fast

Boil the water an' make' a tea

It builds guid bones n' cleans yer pee.

Docken bides tae ease the sting

fae nettles prickly mood

and if ye faw n' cut yirsel

wi' docken bind the wound.

Borage pretty as it is

hides it's face fae ye n' me

but soak it well an' make' a tea

yer skin will clear for aw' tae see.

Chamomile to ease yer tears

An' wash awa' yer night-time fears

Lavender tae clean yer cuts

An' burns fae that camp fire's spits

Mint will calm the worried heart

An' ease yer stomach's wind.

Sage abides tae clear yer mind

An' make' yer thinkin' smart

An' Thyme's the wan ye need tae use

tae fight the germs that kill

an' a' these herbs are guid for ye

so use them as ye will.

Chapter 5

Gypsy families had camped near Glasgow Green for as far back as anyone could remember. Being central, they could go from there to the Borders for tin; to Lanark for gathering and picking fruit or vegetables, to the Ayrshire coast for whelks that they picked from the shores. On their travels, they would buy flour and oats from the mills. Farm work was a good source of income for them too and the farmers appreciated the seasonal labour for root vegetables. The farmers that hired them during the seasons provided fresh fruit and vegetables and they could earn up to eight shillings a week. Money they earned would help them buy food if they ran out of supplies. Life was hard in those days and they spent every daylight hour working and taking advantage of the seasons, but at least travelling families had fresh air and fresh food. They feasted on fish caught in the streams, whelks picked off the shore between September and April, game between October and February and Hares caught for the pot in August after the breeding and nursing cycle was over. They purchased oats, grains, and flour from the mills; kept their own hens for a regular supply of eggs, and milk or cheese came from the nearest dairy farm.

Seasonal farm work was by far the hardest and the happiest of times for the travelling families, whether they were picking turnips, potatoes, or soft fruits. For children this meant meeting up with friends and families and helping their parents. During the picking season it was not uncommon for the families to work from six o'clock in the mornings until late in the evenings, but this was something that everyone looked forward to, adults and children alike, for they were well looked after and well paid by the farmers. If the farms were close by, travelling families would return to their own wagons at night, but if the farms were further afield, whole camps would just gather up their belongings and move to where the work was. Night times were the best of times, for the fine weather meant singing songs round the campfires and sleeping under the stars. There was always a bender to shelter under if the weather was foul. Sometimes a farmhand would arrive at a camp as early as five o'clock in the morning, and everyone would pile into the farmer's cart happy and laughing, ready to go to work. The farmer's wife would have prepared an urn full of tea, and piles of sandwiches, which they would enjoy before they began their shift. There was always enough to feed everyone. At weekends, a big breakfast of home cured bacon, fresh laid eggs, and homemade tattie scones was served. Bread would be thick, crusty, and still warm from the oven, and butter churned fresh would be as yellow as the summer sun. In those days, many farmers made the travellers part of the family, and it was a natural thing for Gypsy children to become friends with farmer's children.

The beginning of June signalled the start of harvesting and everyone would pile into the fields and begin the days' work. Farmers sold the crops they gathered at markets and fairs or to locals who would go direct to them for their produce. Everyone worked side by side with the exception of the teenagers, who liked to work in their own little group, but they worked hard while they talked and giggled. At night, everyone sat around and talked about the days' work before retiring for a good sleep.

The women's role was primarily to mind the home and the children, but they also earned a living by making lace doilies, bunches of Lucky White Heather, Mistletoe and Holly garlands, and Lavender posies. They sold handcrafted items from door to door in nearby towns or villages. Most of them followed the old religion and if they had the gift of second sight, they told housewives their fortunes. Isabella and George's oldest daughters Jennie and Nellie had learned how to crochet little cotton circles for covering jam and honey pots and larger mats for women to set on their sideboards. They often sat of an evening doing this so that they could sell them when they went around doors with their mother.

During winter, the men would gather mistletoe to sell and while they were climbing trees to collect it, the women would be gathering sprigs, ripe with red berries, from the holly trees to make the Christmas decorations. Spring, summer, autumn, or winter, there was always something to do and no hands were ever idle. The young lads would go with their fathers, learning from an early age how to earn a living. Each family had a separate skill set that they were able to earn from, and they would chip in and share whatever they could if another family ran short. After the harsh realities of winter, they always looked forward to attending fairs in Scotland and England and this was a regular feature of life for them. They looked forward to buying goods, selling their crafts, trading horses, dogs, and ferrets, and meeting up with friends or family members who had moved with husbands or wives to live in other camps.

Sickness was rife for home dwellers especially those with children at school, as head lice, scabies, and ringworm, were common. Worse still were mumps, measles, tuberculosis, scarlet fever, whooping cough, and the many other, often fatal, illnesses that plagued them. Children and the elderly were most at risk, the life expectancy for that time was between forty-five and fifty for the poor and manual workers, and the infant mortality rate was very high. Understandably, travelling families tried to stay away from those who were sick, but their life style had penalties too, and they were often harassed for poaching, vagrancy, or trespassing; and if they were caught, harsh prison sentences were imposed on them. One travelling family that fell foul of the authorities was harassed to the point that they were warned that if they didn't move into a permanent home they would have their children taken from them, and they would be put into the 'poor house'. These words were spoken easily from the mouths of those who did not know what struggle was. Those who were in positions of power or authority did not care that finding a home was next to impossible, and for a travelling family, living in one would be like a prison to them.

Chapter 6

Time passed and both girls were beautiful to look at with long jet-black curly hair and deep dark brown eyes. By the time Mary was four, Coralina, then almost twelve, noticed that Mary had something different about her. Sometimes Mary would stop in the middle of things and just stare off into the distance.

"C'mon Mary," Coralina would urge her, "stop yer day dreamin', help me wi' things."

Then Mary would look at Coralina as though she knew something that her big sister didn't. Sometimes Mary would make an announcement like, "Tom's got a sore leg."

Much later, Tom would be seen limping. Coralina had heard the aunties talking about 'The Sight', and she had a vague idea what it meant, but she had never seen it happening before and it had never happened to her. She was a little afraid of it and a little worried.

This went on for some time before Coralina plucked up the courage to speak to Auntie Isabella.

"Dae ye know whit 'The Sight' is Auntie Isabella?"

"Aye, why dae ye ask hinny?"

"Is it bad for ye, can it hurt ye?"

"Why are ye askin' me that hinny?"

"Whit does it mean Auntie Isabella?"

"Is there somethin' ye should be telling me?" Isabella was looking at Coralina who was twisting her hands in agitation.

"Dae ye think ye have seen summat?"

"It's no' me Auntie Isabella, it's our Mary."

"Whit makes ye think she has the sight?"

"She says things."

"Whit kind o' things?"

"Jist stuff, and then it happens. Sometimes she goes quiet and looks,… Ah don't know, jist different."

"It's a rare and precious gift, the gift o' the sight Coralina, yer mother had it. She knew all sorts of things, an' sometimes Ah think she knew way too much."

"But whit does it mean Auntie Isabella?"

"Some people pretend tae have it tae earn a sixpence, some pretend tae have it tae show off an' feel important, but there are some that can see whit's gone afore an' whit's still tae come an' often those that have it can make things happen."

"Whit dae ye mean, like seein' pictures in yer heed?"

"Summat like that, everybody can imagine pictures, but folk that have the sight dinnae imagine them, the pictures just come, an' then the pictures come true."

"Ah don't ken whit tae dae, Ah'm supposed tae look oot for her."

"Ye canny dae onythin' hinny, but Ah'll have a wee word wi' Mither an' we'll see whit she says, dinnae worry yer self Coralina."

The next day Isabella was chatting to her cousin Lizzie, who was married to Arthur Donnelly; he bought and sold pots, pans, stainless steel baths, wash basins, and jugs. They were standing by a fire where a galvi basin full of water was propped over the flames to boil their whites.

"Whit's up wi' ye the day Isabella, ye've a worried look aboot ye," said the Mither as she approached them.

"Ah was jist telling Lizzie aboot a chat Ah had wi' Coralina. She thinks oor Mary has the sight and she's fair feart for her."

"Aye, she has that. She has a power aboot her that Ah huvnae seen the like o' for a while."

"Whit are wi' tae dae Mither?"

"Nuthin ye can dae, 'cept teach her right from wrang and how tae mind her ain business."

"Coralina says Mary sees things and tells her aboot them afore they happen," said Isabella.

"Ah never mentioned afore," said Lizzie, "but Ah've heard her an' it's a wee bit scary, she gets a look aboot her before she says summat, an' Ah'm aye feart o' whit she's gonnae tell us."

"Aye, it can be a curse or a blessin," said the Mither, "Ah'll keep an eye on her."

Mary's nature was changing; where Coralina was a sensible, obliging, child who always had a ready smile, Mary often displayed a mean side when she didn't get her own way. Coralina did all that was expected of her, but often when she asked for help, Mary would just give her a look and walk away. Coralina lavished love and attention on Mary, as did everyone else, but gradually Mary was gaining a reputation of being selfish and spoiled. Mary was not slow about lifting her hand and striking another child, and no matter what Coralina said or did, Mary was a law unto herself. Coralina didn't want to tell her father but as time passed Mary's behaviour and attitude grew worse. Eventually Coralina spoke to her father.

"She cannae be trusted Da, if ye tell her tae dae summat she only does it if it suits her, and she's got a vicious streak. She punched wee Daisy an' bled her lip, an' Auntie Isabella was ragin'. She tells lies an' a' when she gets caught daein' summat she blames wan o' the cousins."

John sighed sadly, he too had noticed the changes in Mary, and he blamed himself for being too soft on her. He missed Mary Ellen more than ever and silently sent up a prayer to his wife for guidance.

"Dinnae worry Coralina, Ah'll have a word wi' her an' see if she can mend her ways. We've an early start in the morn to head for the Dalgarven Mill. Ah'll speak tae her the morra'. Ah've some horses tae shift an' we'll bring some flour an' oats back."

Coralina felt the better for having shared her worries about Mary with her father, and she went to sleep that night with hope in her heart, and a sense of excitement too, for she liked going to Dalgarven Mill better than anywhere. They had been going there regularly for as long as she could remember. For summer trips, they left the wagon at the camp and took a big cart and if it was a long trip, they camped beside it in benders. In colder months, they took the wagon and carried a small flat bed trailer, which was stowed under the wagon. They would re-assemble it, fill it with provisions, and tow it behind them as needed. Coralina loved sitting up in the front of the cart with the sun shining on them as they travelled. She would sing old songs and Mary would join in singing and laughing,

"Be baw babbity, babbity, babbity, be baw babbity, kiss the bonnie wee lassie."

They stopped at various farms along the way and while her father attended to the business of selling and buying horses, they would be playing in the sun and singing their favourite songs. For Coralina, every trip to Ayrshire started with an eager anticipation because she had made friends with the miller's son Robert, and she was always happy to see him when they reached Dalgarven Mill. Robert was a little bit taller than she was and had thick fair hair and blue eyes. She smiled to herself as she thought about the way his hair stuck up at the crown of his head, and how he always tried to flatten it. She liked the way it stuck up, but she knew that when she saw him coming towards the wagon the first thing he would do was put his hand up and flatten the unruly tuft. Sometimes Robert and she would wander down by the banks of the River Garnock and play for a while on the sandbank and then it would be back to the mill for a bite to eat before they began their journey home.

Chapter 7

John Kelly always maintained about ten to twelve horses at a time. He had four for pulling the cart or the wagon. Just two horses pulled the cart on short journeys, but on longer trips, John would have two horses leading and two spare horses on guide ropes. From time to time on long journeys, he would swop the horses over to give them a rest from pulling a heavy load. He kept his other horses for breeding, trading at the horse fairs, or selling to farmers. John had a reputation for knowing all there was to know about breeding the best working horses, known as Vanners. Some would say he had an instinct for looking at a foal and knowing that she would be a great brood mare, or a colt, and knowing that he would sire the best horses for pulling wagons. This trip to Ayrshire was an important one because he already had orders for a few of his horses and he planned to keep his eyes open just in case he came across a fine filly or two to breed. He could make a pairing of filly and foal that would later produce a Vanner that was not only a good worker or breeder, but was also a thing of beauty to be admired and shown off at the horse fairs.

Gypsy Vanners were beautiful horses to look at with their long feathered manes that came almost half way down their bodies. They were a joy to observe when they were trotting or cantering, amusing themselves in the fields, or when they were being ridden fast by the young lads showing off at the various fairs. Thick tails, strong fetlocks, and beautifully coloured coats set them apart from other plainer breeds. Little did anyone know that much, much later, when the war would break out, that these colourful flashy horses would be spared being taken to the front line because of their bright colours.

One of his prime concerns was temperament, and he specialised in rearing horses that were not only powerful, but gentle natured. Even the smallest children were safe on a Vanner. Each day he would take the horses one by one, and exercise and groom them. He would brush their long manes and tails and generally handle them so that they were comfortable around people. He would whisper quietly to them and give them an occasional treat of a piece of carrot or turnip, and they loved him in return. They could sense when he was approaching, picking up their ears and then pointing them forward to welcome his approach. When he handed over his treat, a soft nicker would reward him. One by one, he would go round each horse in turn, running his hands down their legs, and feeling their muscles and tendons. Any sign of heat or swelling would mean that there was a strain or injury and that would need tending to immediately by applying a wrap of cabbage leaves or a mash of Chamomile to ease and reduce any inflammation.

John's cousin and best friend Willie McGuigan had four sons. Three of them were always to be found by their fathers side no matter what he was doing, but his youngest son Johnny, who was two years older than Mary, loved being around the horses, and he was always hanging about his Uncle John. Whenever John went to feed and care for the horses young Johnny wasn't far behind him with his father Willie's words ringing in his ears.

"Don't get under yer Uncle John's feet mind."

"Ah won't Da," would reply the youngster.

Since John had no sons, young Johnny's presence was a delight to him, and he enjoyed explaining what he was doing with the horses, and teaching him how to look after and care for them.

Although she had no need to be jealous, Mary hated the attention that her father gave to young Johnny, and she was often spiteful towards him. Johnny was better natured though, he seldom let Mary's nasty side bother him, and soon, when she realised that Johnny didn't react to her jibes, she stopped bothering him. Before long, young Johnny became an extension to the family and, as on this occasion, John would have a word with Willie.

"Ah'm off in the morning to Ayrshire wi' some horses and bringin' back some provisions. Ah'll take young Johnny if ye dinnae need him for onythin'?"

Willie laughed in response, "He'll moan a' day if Ah say he cannae go. Johnny loves bein' wi' his Uncle John an' the horses."

The next day, at the break of dawn, they were all up dressed, and making their way through Glasgow towards Ayrshire. They would travel about fifty or so miles on this journey, managing fifteen miles each day, with just a few short breaks to feed and rest the horses, and to have something to eat. They would be going to some Ayrshire farms to deliver horses ending up at Dalgarven Mill. Each night they would stop at a suitable place and while John unhitched and saw to the horses, Coralina would unload the tarpaulin and hazel poles so that her father could set up the bender where they would sleep. They always camped in the same places, near streams for fresh water for the horses and for cooking and washing.

John would loosely tether the horses allowing them to graze then he would begin putting the bender together. While he was busy with that, Mary and young Johnny fetched twigs to start the fire and Coralina would set some stones in a circle to contain it and then fetch the kettle to hang over the chitty prop. With the fire lit, and a good flame going, John would hang the kettle over so that they could brew some tea.

This became the pattern with John, Coralina, Mary, and young Johnny travelling around Ayrshire together. John was happy having young Johnny around because he seemed to have a calming influence on Mary. Over time,

Mary stopped needling Johnny and then just watched him wherever he went. Her eyes followed him, and occasionally he would look up and smile at her, and she would just draw him a look and turn her back, but before long, she would be watching him again. Mary even began to chat to Johnny. At first it was just questions, 'Why are you doing this or that or where are you going?' Johnny was always polite and even-tempered, and soon Mary realised that she got more attention, nicer attention, when she was polite, than the attention she got, or lack of it, when she was being mean. The mean streak was still there but it did not show itself as much.

Often while Coralina and her father were sitting up at the front of the cart, she would glance across to him, and he would glance back at her and smile, as both knowingly acknowledged that Mary and Johnny were chatting in the back. It was nice to hear them talking, nicer still that Mary was being friendly rather than sullen. The motion of the wagon as it rolled over the uneven roads often lulled the youngsters to sleep but Coralina was too excited to sleep. She had other things on her mind. Coralina was twelve now nearly thirteen and she was beginning to feel quite grown up. Since she did everything that a grown woman did, this was really no surprise, but there was still innocence to her and that in itself was appealing to those who knew her.

Coralina began to think of the Millers of Dalgarven Mill, they were a lovely family and they always had a bite to eat ready for them whenever they arrived. They always made sure that they had something to eat before they left, often giving them a loaf of crusty bread and some cheese or scones to take away with them. Elsie and Mathew were their names, and typical of country folk, they rose early in the day and worked until late in the evening. Running a mill was hard responsible work, as they provided for the needs of everyone in the local area, nevertheless they made time for their visitors. Coralina began to think about Robert and she found herself wondering if he would kiss her, and then she was horrified at the thought. Her cheeks flushed with embarrassment as she realised what she was thinking.

"Are ye a'right lass? … Coralina! Ah'm speakin' tae ye, are ye feelin a'right?"

Coralina jumped guiltily as she realised that her father was speaking to her. "Aye Da, Ah'm fine."

"Ye look a bit flushed hinny, are ye sure yer ok?"

"Ah'm fine Da, honest."

She knew her father would be furious if he thought she was thinking about things like that. She wondered where the thought had come from because she had never thought of anything like that before, but the more she tried to put it out of her mind the more it popped back in again.

These were happy days for all concerned but no one could possibly anticipate what was to come, except Mary that is. She was already seeing pictures in her mind and although she couldn't fully understand them, she didn't like them. She didn't like them one little bit, and this of course altered her mood and her behaviour.

Chapter 8

Often, when they arrived at the mill, Mathew would appear, his hair dusted grey with a fine layer of flour, and a happy grin on his face as he welcomed them, his floury hand outstretched to shake John's. He would have a smile and a word for the girls and young Johnny. Elsie was always busy doing something, feeding chickens, seeing to the few cows that they kept for milking, and sometimes she would greet them, her face red from the heat of the bread oven. She would usher them into the cosy kitchen to sit at a table laden with homemade bread, freshly churned butter, fresh jam, and scones straight from the oven in the big black range.

While John and Mathew looked at the horses and talked business, young Johnny was hanging on every word, taking on board everything that he heard, and learning from his mentor. Mary on the other hand was sitting under a tree in a sulk because no one was paying her any heed, and Coralina had gone down to the side of the mill where she could sit by the stream in the afternoon sun and watch the mill wheel turning as it was pushed by the strong flow of water. Mary could see Coralina from where she was sitting and she saw Robert going over to sit beside her. The pair of them chatted for a while and then Robert, leaning towards Coralina, reached his hand over, touched her hair, said something to her, and Coralina smiled at him with her cheeks turning pink. Mary watched the interaction between the two, and was overwhelmed with a feeling that she couldn't explain. Coralina was hers. She didn't want Robert or anyone else being her friend. She closed her eyes tight, her anger building up inside and her thoughts racing, *"Ah hate him, he shouldnae be touchin' ma sister."* Suddenly she heard a yell, and looked over to see Robert sitting on the ground, holding his wrist and Coralina fussing over him. He had slipped off the wall and landed badly on his hand. Coralina looked over, sensing Mary watching, and she saw her smile at what had happened.

"Away in tae the kitchen an' let yer Mam have a look at that, it might need a poultice Robert."

Coralina hurried over to Mary, "Ah saw ye smirking Mary, and Ah think yer badness is wrang. Ah think ye make things happen wi' yer badness, Ah dinnae ken how, but Ah'm sure its summat ye did."

Mary kept her eyes down but inside she was sad, she didn't want Coralina to be angry with her. She loved Coralina, but she didn't know what to say to her to make things right. Coralina sat under the tree beside her and put her arm around Mary's shoulder. "Talk tae me Mary. Whatever is up wi' ye? Ah know ye can dae things, an' Ah know ye can see things, but ye cannae hurt people."

Mary began to cry, she was confused and frightened and sorry that the thing had happened. She leaned in to Coralina and hid her face in Coralina's chest.

"Can ye talk tae me aboot it Mary?"

"Ah don't know, it jist happens sometimes, if Ah get angry."

"Whit happens Mary?"

"Ah don't know; Ah don't know whit it is."

"Look, here comes Robert, dinnae say anythin' tae him, I like him Mary, he's ma friend."

Mary reached up and hugged Coralina as Robert approached.

"Is yer hand ok Robert?"

"Aye its fine, Coralina, it was jist a bit sore when it happened. Yer Da says tae tell ye that he's waiting for ye."

"Thanks Robert," said Coralina.

"Ah'll see ye the next time then?"

"Aye Robert, we'll be back soon enough."

The sacks of flour and oats were stowed in the wagon, and John was shaking Mathews hand as the girls approached. Elsie came out drying her hands on a tea towel.

"Thanks very much Missus Miller," said Coralina, and she gave Mary a small nudge.

"Thanks Missus Miller, it was nice to be here," said Mary.

Young Johnny piped in with, "Ah might see ye again Missus."

"Ah'm sure ye will Johnny, Ah'm sure ye will," laughed Mrs Miller.

They climbed up on to the cart piled high with sacks of oats and wheat and waved to the Millers as they set off to their camp for the night. It would be an early rise for them to head back home, and it would be late when they got there. The journey home was uneventful, apart from the fact that Coralina was preoccupied with worrying thoughts of Mary and what she might be capable of. She didn't really understand, and although she wanted to ask Mither Morrison, she was a bit afraid of doing so, because she didn't know what the Mither would say or do about it. She wondered if it was just a coincidence that Robert fell off the small wall and hurt himself, and then again maybe it wasn't.

The rolling of the wagon had lulled Johnny and Mary off to sleep.

“Yer quiet hinny,” her Da said, “is there summat troubling ye?”

“Well…”

“Speak up lass.”

“It’s just, ye know Ah'm the nearest thing tae a Mam that oor Mary has.”

“Aye.”

“Well its jist that a want tae dae the right thing by her.”

“Ah ken she can be a bit o’ a handful, but ye dae a guid job wi’ her Coralina, an’ yer Mam would be so proud o’ ye, but if yer worried ye know ye can aye ask me or Auntie Isabella or the Mither. Is there summat ye want tae tell me?”

“Naw Da, Ah think Ah'll speak tae Auntie Isabella.”

John was quiet for the rest of the journey, as was Coralina, both engrossed in their thoughts. John wondering if there was something he should know or something he could do better, and Coralina wondering if she would be doing the right thing by expressing her fears to her aunt or the Mither.

They made good time on the journey home, stopping only once on the road, and they were all ready for something to eat before they got settled down for the night and feasted on tea and the scones Elsie had given them before they left. The next day would be a busy one for John, as he would share out the provisions that he had purchased for the rest of the camp. The horses would be rubbed down, watered, and fed, then allowed to rest after their journey. Before long it would be time to go back on the road again. For Coralina it was a different story; she had made up her mind to speak to her aunt again and that was the first thing on her mind when she woke up.

In those days, marrying outside the Gypsy culture was frowned upon, more so even than in present times. Travelling families were expected to marry within their own culture. It was common for them to marry as young as fourteen or fifteen and to marry first or second cousins. Since they lived in small tight knit groups, keeping themselves to themselves, marrying outside their own community was rare. Families could be torn apart by such an event and those that considered this option would bring shame and disgrace on their family. Gypsy men were aggressively protective of their women and they would go to almost any lengths to prevent such a thing from happening, it just wasn't tolerated.

"Mornin' lass, did ye have a good trip tae Dalgarven?"

"Aye Auntie Isabella, ma Da sold the horses we took wi' us and wi' finished up at the mill. Missus Miller fed us well, an' Ah saw Robert."

The moment Roberts name was out of her mouth she blushed. Isabella, canny as ever, knew there was more to come, but waited to see if Coralina would be forthcoming, or if she would need prompted. There was silence as Coralina stood looking uncomfortable, and Isabella carried on with her chores until after a bit she said, "Let's go sit by the fire an' have a drink o' tea." Isabella lifted the heavy kettle from its hook as Coralina put the teapot on a wooden box by the fire. Isabella poured the water into the teapot and added a small handful of leaves. They both sat quietly for a few moments, Isabella waiting, and Coralina trying to find the right words to begin.

"Roberts nice."

"Aye, Ah've heard yer Da sayin' that they're a nice family."

"He stroked ma hair."

"Did he now?" Isabella said, raising her eyebrows.

Coralina continued in a rush, "The thing is Auntie Isabella, Mary was watchin' from under the trees an' Robert fell off the wall, it was jist a wee wall, an' he jist slipped right aff it, an' Ah think it was oor Mary made him fa'."

For a moment Isabella almost laughed, and then she remembered the conversation she had with the Mither about the sight sometimes being a gift or a curse. She pressed her lips together waiting to see if there was more.

"She's jealous Auntie Isabella, she disnae like me bein' too friendly wi' anybody. Ah tried tae talk tae her, an' she feels guilty, so it must ha' been her.

"Was he bad hurt?"

"Naw no' really, jist a sprain in his wrist, he's a' right but Ah'm worried aboot Mary."

"Drink yer tea Coralina an' dinnae worry yer self, Ah'll have a word wi' the Mither."

"Thanks Auntie Isabella."

"So tell me about Robert?"

"Aw he's nice Auntie Isabella, I like him."

Isabella didn't say anything, she would talk to the Mither, about this as well as what to do about young Mary.

Chapter 9

Later that day the Mither and Isabella sat discussing what Coralina had revealed.

"Whit did ye say tae her Isabella?"

"Ah jist told her that Ah'd have a word wi' ye."

"Aye, its wan tae think aboot," the Mither said, shaking her head worriedly. "The problem wi' Mary is wan thing, but Coralina needs tae mind that she cannae be too close tae Gorja's. She has tae stick tae her ain kind. Ah'll have a think aboot this an' Ah might need tae have a word wi' John tae. He'll no' be happy if he has tae hear this."

A few days later the Mither called young Mary to her side, "C'mon take a walk wi' me Mary." She took Mary's hand in hers and began to lead her away from the camp,

"Whur are wi' goin' Mither."

"Jist a walk hinny, an' maybe a wee seat by the Clyde."

It was nice day, the early morning sun was shining, and the birds were singing in the trees above them. As they reached the old log that was a favourite seat for everyone, the Mither leaned on Mary's shoulder as she eased herself down.

"Sit aside me lass," she said patting the log for Mary to join her.

Mary was worried, she sensed that something was coming but she wasn't sure what it would be.

"Aye we've had many a chat on oor walks hinny."

Mary was silent.

"Whit dae ye see aboot ye Mary?"

"Whit dae ye mean Mither?"

"Ah mean whit Ah say, whit dae ye think Ah mean?"

"Ah don't ken Mither."

"Jist look aboot ye an' tell me whit ye see."

Mary took a breath and looked around, "Ah see the river Mither, an' the grass an' the trees, is that whit ye mean?"

"Aye Ah mean that, an' whit can ye tell me about a' that hinny?"

"It's aye here?" she questioned.

"Aye its aye here an' that's 'cause it lives Mary. It lives 'cause wi' dinnae damage it."

"Ah dinnae ken whit ye mean Mither."

"Everythin' ye see aboot ye has life in it Mary, it's like the music, ye kin hear it but ye cannae see it."

Mary sat and thought for a few moments, and the Mither waited and watched the child thinking and then Mary said, "So when ma Mam died did her music stop?"

"Naw hinny it didnae stop, it jist played somewhere else. The music was inside her an' when her body died the music left its shell an' floated free."

"Is it still floatin'?"

"Aye, an' that's why sometimes ye can see stuff, yer like yer mother."

Mary turned suddenly with her mouth open in surprise and looked at the Mither. There they sat the wise old woman and the innocent child meeting a moment of awareness.

"Ah didnae ken ye knew Ah could see stuff Mither."

"Aye Ah kent, yer Mam could see stuff an' a'."

"She could see the music?"

"Ye could say that."

This was a lot to think about for Mary, part of her was excited that she was the same as her mother, while another part was a little wary that the Mither knew. She had so many questions but didn't know where to start.

"Ye see Mary, sometimes people that can see the music can dae harm as well as guid' if they're no' careful an' they dinnae know what they're daein'. Ah think maybe you might be a wee bit like that."

"Ah dinnae ken whit ye mean Mither."

"Ye've heard yer Uncle Willie playin' the fiddle?"

Mary was confused, "Aye."

"An' it makes a grand sound?" said the Mither.

"Aye."

"Whit would happen if a string broke Mary?"

Mary almost fell backwards laughing at just such a memory, "Aw it sounds jist terrible, Ah remember when that happened before an' Uncle Willie was ragin."

"That's whit Ah mean Mary, when ye damage summat ye break the music."

Mary sat and looked up at the Mither as realisation came to her, and then the tears began to fall. "Ah think Ah broke Robert's music."

The Mither put her arm over Mary's shoulder and Mary leaned in accepting the comfort, but still she cried. "Ye damaged his music Mary. He's a'right noo, but it's worse than that, ye see whit goes aroon comes aroon, so ye need tae remember that, an' if ye stop an' think aboot it ye damaged Coralina's music tae 'cause everythin's connected."

"Whit dae ye mean Mither?"

"It's like throwin' a wee stone in the river, get a wee stone an' throw it in an' tell me whit ye see."

Mary looked about for a bit and then picked up a stone and threw it in the water. She and the Mither watched as the stone landed with a loud plop. Then Mary looked at the Mither.

"Dae ye see the ripples Mary?"

"Aye Ah see them."

"Well the stone landed in the middle o' the water but the ripples keep comin, dae ye see them comin right back tae the edge here?"

"Aye Ah see them, Ah never noticed that before."

"When ye dae summat bad, the ripples keep movin' until they come back tae ye. Ye can dae guid wi' yer gift, but ye can dae harm tae. Dae guid an' guid things will aye come tae ye, but be sure o' this Mary, if ye dae summat bad it's the hardest thing tae take back, and bad will come right back at ye when ye least expect it."

"Ah'm feart Mither."

Once more, the Mither gave Mary a comforting squeeze, "An' so ye should be hinny, so ye should be. Aye be good an' good will come tae ye."

"Is summat bad gonnae happen tae me Mither?"

"Only if yer no' careful aboot whit ye dae. Ye see yer gift is like the music, if you play a nice tune, ye make people happy an' that makes ye happy. Ye have strong music Mary. Put yer hand out."

Mary put out her hand and the Mither placed her hand above it. "Can ye feel that Mary," she asked.

"Ah feel heat Mither, is that whit ye mean?"

"That's yer music Mary, an' yer music is strong enough tae heal Mary. Yer body is jist a shell tae haud the music, it's the music that gives ye life, it's yer energy."

Mary eyes were wide with amazement, "Ye mean Ah can make a body well when they're sick?"

"Sometimes Mary, but no' a' the time. Sometimes people are meant tae pass on, jist like yer Mam did when she went tae be wi' the angels, but if yer a guid lass an' yer careful whit ye dae ye might be able tae help people instead o' troublin' them."

"Ah think Johnny has good music Mither."

"Aye, yer right, Johnny has got good music an' ye should be nice tae him."

"Ah will Mither, thanks for helpin me."

"Help me up an' we'll go back tae the camp."

Mary was like a different person as they approached the camp; she was smiling and running ahead of the Mither and then running back to have a quick word, only to repeat the process over and over again. Isabella, watching for them coming, breathed a sigh of relief. She could see the Mither laughing at Mary's antics and Mary seemed so happy. It was obvious that the talk had gone well.

Chapter 10

The kettle had come to the boil, and Isabella made a fresh pot of tea for her and the Mither.

"Sit yer self doon Mither an' have some tea."

"Thanks Isabella, that was nae bad, Ah think she understands but time'll tell. Ah didnae have tae let on that Ah kent aboot the wee accident wi' Robert, for she brought his name up hersel'."

"Whit aboot Coralina and Robert, will ye say summat tae Coralina or will ye say summit tae oor John?"

"Does Coralina ken aboot her body changing?"

"Ah dinnae think so,"

"Will ye have a word wi' her Isabella?"

"Me! No' me, Ah'm embarris'd tae mention that," said Isabella her face turning red at the thought. "Ah'll tell oor Jennie tae speak tae her aboot it."

"It's up tae ye Isabella, but after me yer the oldest an' ye'll be the Mither when Ah'm no' here an' ye'll need tae take responsibility then."

"Wheesht, Ah'll no' hear oh that."

"When it's ma' time, its ma' time, nuthin' onybody kin dae aboot that."

Just at that moment, Coralina came over to the fire. Always polite and respectful she said, "Mither, Auntie Isabella, can Ah come an' sit by ye."
"Aye, sit Coralina, have ye summat on yer mind?"

"Ah jist wanted tae tell ye that Mary seems awfy happy. Ah'm guessin' ye had a word wi' her Mither."

"Ah did that, an Ah think she understood."

"Ah'm ever so grateful Mither, Ah'm sure she will be a'right noo, thanks."

Later that day Jennie came over to seek her out.

"What are ye up tae Coralina?"

"Nuthin' much how?"

"Jist wanted a word."

"Aye, whit?"

"Aw well, ye see ma Mam wanted me tae speak tae ye about changin'."

"Changin' whit?"

"Ye ken?"

"Ah don't ken whit yer talkin' aboot."

"Ah'm talkin' aboot changin' fae a lassie tae a wummin."

"Dae ye mean like the animals when the bitches are ready an' they go into the heat an' the blood comes?"

"Are ye takin' a rise? Ye should ha' said ye kent."

"Well, Ah jist know aboot the animal's fae whit Ah've seen."

"Aye, it's the same as that, an' ye cannae let a fella near ye, it'll shame ye an' shame yer family, an' ye have tae keep yer self clean an' stay away fae Gorjas."

"Some Gorjas are a'right."

"Naw Coralina, stay away fae them 'cause ye might get tempted tae be wi' wan, and that would be the end, so jist take a tellin'." With that, not prepared to discuss the matter any further, Jennie turned and walked away leaving Coralina to her thoughts about becoming a woman.

Mary was a different girl after the chat with the Mither. Her behaviour changed considerably, but she still had moments when she lost her way and forgot the lesson the Mither had taught her, but as soon as she remembered, for fear of something bad happening to her, she would try to make amends to anyone that she had scorned. She helped Coralina without too much persuasion, and even young Johnny felt the benefit of this new Mary. Coralina was happier that she had ever been, and that summer was one of the best that she remembered.

Autumn and winter came and went, and soon the daffodils were blooming and everyone was looking forward to getting out on the road and visiting old friends and families once more. Unbeknown to Coralina, who had celebrated her thirteenth birthday, the Mither had had a word with John about Coralina's friendship with Robert, the Miller's son, and at the end of the discussion, they agreed to put some distance between Coralina and Robert.

The first Coralina knew about it was when her father was getting ready to make the first of his trips to Ayrshire and the Dalgarven Mill.

"Ah'm jist takin young Johnny, you'll bide here wi' yer sister and mind the Mither for she's getting on in years."

Never one to answer back Coralina shocked John when she retorted "But Da!"

John turned his head quickly and glowered at Coralina, and she hung her head, but she wasn't happy and she wasn't finished.

"Ah've worked hard a' winter Da, Ah was really lookin' furrat tae goin tae Ayrshire wi' ye."

"Ye'll bide here Coralina, an' Ah'll brook nae argument on the matter."

Coralina ran outside and across the camp towards the river, and when she got there she sat on the log, put her face in her hands, and cried. She started when someone placed a hand on her shoulder.

"Whit's up wi' ye Coralina, why are ye greetin'?" Mary sat beside her sister and she had a fretful expression on her young face; she had never seen her cry like that.

"It's ma Da, he says Ah cannae go tae Ayrshire wi' him."

"Am Ah goin'?"

"Yer no' goin' either."

"Whit aboot Johnny, is he goin'?"

"Aye he's goin', but we have tae stay and mind the Mither. Ah think that's jist an excuse, but Ah dinnae ken why he would dae that."

Mary sat quiet but she wasn't happy either. Over time, she and Johnny had become good friends, and she hadn't once felt that burning jealousy when her father paid Johnny attention, but she felt it now and it troubled her. She jumped up and ran away back to the camp. She saw Johnny making his way towards the horse's field.

"Johnny, Johnny," she called.

Hearing her call, Johnny turned with a smile on his face, but it quickly vanished when he saw her agitation and he hurried towards her.

"Whit's up Mary?"

"Are ye gone tae Ayrshire wi' ma Da?"

"Aye!" he answered in surprise, and without a thought, Mary kicked him on the shin and stomped off. She was quickly yanked back when Johnny grabbed her by the shoulder. Mary was shocked, and so was Johnny, though he didn't show it, for he had always been taught to be gentle with girls.

"Whit did ye dae that for Mary, Ah thought ye were past that stuff, look at ma leg Mary, look at whit ye have done. Ye've skint ma shin," he said as he rolled up his trousers and viewed the graze.

Mary's eyes were full of tears as she looked down at Johnny's leg, but her tears were there for selfish reasons. She was thinking about the consequences of her actions. She had lost her temper again, and done something to hurt someone.

"Ah'm sorry Johnny, Ah didnae mean it."

"Whit dae ye mean ye didnae mean it, did your foot jist connect wi' ma leg?"

Mary laughed, "Yer so funny Johnny."

However, Johnny didn't laugh, and Mary's laugh was quickly smothered as she clamped her lips tightly together, her eyes suddenly filled with tears.

"Aye, Ah might be, but you're no' funny Mary, you're no' funny at a'."

Johnny turned his back on Mary and walked away from her.

"Johnny Ah'm sorry, honest," said Mary as she ran after him, but Johnny was having none of it.

Disgusted with herself, Mary went back to where she had left Coralina and sat beside her. She slipped her hand into her big sister's and the two of them sat there absorbed in their own misery.

Chapter 11

Later Coralina went to see her aunt, "Whit's up wi' ye the day Coralina, it's no' like ye tae be doon in the dumps."

"Mam, Da says Ah cannae go tae Ayrshire wi' him, that me an' Mary have tae bide here."

Isabella knew the reason behind this but wasn't prepared to share it with Coralina.

"He says Ah've tae look after the Mither."

"She's no' so able these days Coralina, Ah'm sure ye don't mind really."

"Ah'm disappointed."

"Ah'm sure ye are hinny, but maybe ye'll get tae go another day."

Coralina thought about Robert. He had been in her mind a lot recently and she was looking forward to seeing him, then she wondered if he was looking forward to seeing her. There was nothing else for it but to get on with things, so she accepted the inevitable and said no more about it, but inside, she felt miserable and unhappy.

Her Da and young Johnny left for Ayrshire early the next day. Coralina and Mary watched them ride off on the wagon until they couldn't see them anymore. Mary had hoped for a wave from Johnny, but he was still annoyed with her and didn't turn his head.

For the next few days Isabella kept a watch over both girls and Coralina did as her father had bid her, and went over to the Mithers a few times each day to see if she needed anything and to take her cups of tea and some dinner.

"How are ye feeling Mither?"

"Ah'm a bit sore an' stiff Coralina, but there's nowt a buddy kin dae aboot that. Ah've a cabbage poultice on ma knees that could be warmed up if ye have a mind tae take it across tae the fire?"

Coralina waited while the Mither hitched up her woollen skirt and rolled down her thick stockings, and then she helped her to unwrap the poultice.

"Ah'll make ye a new wan Mither."

"Yer a guid lass Coralina, ye remind me a lot of yer Mam, and yer jist as lovely as she was."

It was while her father and Johnny were away on their Ayrshire trip that Coralina's body started the change. She woke in the night with bad pains in her stomach and she felt as though her back was breaking. She curled herself up into a tight ball, clutching her belly and the warmth of her hands started to ease her pain. Finally, she fell into a deep sleep, but when she woke early in the morning, she knew something was wrong. As soon as she saw the blood she had a moments panic, and then she realised what was happening to her. She pulled the bed sheet off the bed and rolled it into a ball to hide the bloodstains, before hurrying across to her aunt's wagon.

"Auntie Isabella?"

"Come away in hinny," said Isabella, and then as she saw Coralina's bundle she realised her predicament.

"Ah've started Auntie Isabella, an' Ah'm no' sure whit tae dae."

Isabella overcame her embarrassment and took charge.

"Come wi' me lass," she said as she rummaged in a drawer for some clean rags.

Coralina, meek, uncomfortable, and self-conscious, followed Isabella across the camp towards the river. Isabella led her downstream to a secluded part of the river and began to show her how to take care of herself.

"If ye get any blood on yer sheet rinse it aff doon stream like this."

Isabella shook out the sheet, placed a corner of it on a flat rock, and secured it in place with another on top of it. She loosened out the folds so that the water would run through the marks removing the bulk of the stains.

"Now stand in the shallows here, crouch doon and wipe yer self clean, then dry yer' self wi' this cloth, an' when yer done put wan o' these rags in yer knickers. Ah'll leave ye until yer done, then come back tae mine. Wring oot yer sheet an' bring it wi' ye an' we'll get it in tae the boil."

Isabella left her, and when Coralina was finished, she took her sheet, wrung out as best she could, back to her aunt's wagon.

"Jist leave it under the step the noo an' come in, Ah'll boil it later."

"Thanks for helpin me Auntie Isabella."

"Jennie tells me ye know whit's happenin', but did she tell ye that yer a wummin once that happens? Dae ye ken that ye kin make bairns noo?"

"Well, Ah dinnae have a husband so Ah cannae make bairns."

"Naw, naw, Coralina, ye dinnae need a husband tae make a bairn. Ye have tae be awfy careful noo that ye have changed. Ye cannae let a fella near ye.

Oor kind will have respect for ye, but others, they'll no' care an' would take advantage."

Coralina sat and thought about what her aunt was telling her. "Ah think Ah'm feart Auntie Isabella, whit happens if a fella touches me, will Ah have a bairn?"

"If a fella tries tae kiss ye, and puts his airms aboot ye…then that could be the start o' trouble, so dinnae let it happen, an' keep away fae gorjas."

While Isabella rummaged in a trunk, Coralina thought about what she had said about gorjas. She thought about Robert, because he was a gorja not a Gypsy. She wondered if her Da hadn't taken her because he thought she liked Robert, and was worried that Robert would touch her. '*Naw, Robert was a nice lad an' her Da liked him*,' she thought to herself.

Isabella had pulled an old sheet from the trunk, "Here, take that across tae yer wagon and tear it intae squares. Hide them somewhere an change every time ye go for a pee. Fold one up, stick it in yer knickers, an' wash the rag that ye've used. Wash them how a showed ye an' dinnae let anybody see them dryin', its private."

"Thanks Auntie Isabella."

"Jist as well ye never went tae Ayrshire wi' yer Da or ye would ha' been caught oot."

Coralina's face went bright red as she thought that maybe her Da knew that she was going to change and that was why he didn't take her. The next few days were difficult for Coralina as she was plagued with stomach cramps and on one of the days, Mary went to look for her and was startled to find her lying on the bed in the wagon.

"Whit are ye dayin' lyin' doon, are ye sick Coralina?" asked a worried Mary.

"Ah'm fine Mary, Ah've jist got a sore stomach."

""Whit gave ye a sore stomach, did ye eat summat bad?"

Coralina had to think for a few moments of how to respond, she wondered if she should just avoid the question or if she should just tell Mary what was what. She decided on the latter and if Mary asked questions, she would tell her the truth. "Ah didnae eat summat bad Mary, Ah'm changing from a lassie tae a wummin."

"How long does that take?" asked Mary innocently.

In spite of the cramps Coralina laughed. "It's happened already Mary. Jist like the animals, Ah'm bleedin and Ah'll bleed every month."

"Oh," replied Mary, and then after a little while, standing looking at her sister she said "An' ye get a sore stomach wi' it?"

"Aye."

"Ah' dinnae think Ah would like that Coralina."

"Ye've no' got any choice, it happens tae a' lassies."

"Can Ah try summat Ah've been practisin'?"

"Whit is it ye want tae try?"

"Ah want tae try tae take away yer pain."

Coralina looked at her and then she said "Whit makes ye think ye can dae that."

"The Mither said Ah had good strong music an' if Ah use it right Ah could help people, let me try."

"Ah dinnae ken whit yer talkin' aboot."

"It disnae matter, jist let me try."

"Hurry up then whatever it is yer gonnae dae, get on wi' it."

Mary knelt beside her sister and placed her hands on her stomach and the two girls just stayed like that for several minutes. Mary was aware of the heat building in her hands and she was sure that there was a tingling feeling. Coralina moaned once or twice but Mary stayed as she was, and soon, Coralina began to drift into a contented sleep. When Mary was sure that her sister was sound, she quietly stood, leaned over her, and kissed her cheek. She went outside, sat on the wagon steps, and thought about what had just happened. In her heart, she felt that she had somehow made a difference and she liked that feeling. She promised herself that she would try to help anyone who was sick or sad. It was a much better feeling than the one that consumed her when she was angry or spiteful.

Chapter 12

Young Robert Miller saw John's wagon approaching and ran into the farmhouse to let his mother know, and then he went over to the mill to give his father a shout. He tried hard to contain his excitement and it was only when he walked out with his father that the smile dropped from his face as he realised that neither Coralina nor Mary were on the wagon.

Robert was fifteen now and he had been thinking a lot about Coralina. There were local girls who lived in the village and they were nice lassies, but none could compare with Coralina. He had been looking forward to seeing her and chatting to her, though he would never have admitted that he had a crush on her. Mary was another matter though; she could be a bit of a pest but he would happily put up with Mary for the pleasure of seeing Coralina. His father shed light on their absence.

"Ye didnae bring the lassies wi' ye John?"

"Plenty for them tae dae back yonder Mathew."

"The Missus will miss them; she likes chattin' tae them."

Robert didn't want to show his disappointment, in fact, he didn't want to show his interest in case anyone chided him, so he kept quiet, but he thought about Coralina all day long. It was as though the fact that she wasn't there made his need to see her even stronger, but there was nothing that he could do about that.

Elsie Miller was as hospitable as usual, and after John and Johnny had eaten, they went over to the mill to load up the wagon with flour and oatmeal. Johnny and Robert helped the men and listened while they chatted.

"Where are ye off tae next John?"

"Ah'm gonnae look at some mares just up by Stewarton and Dunlop. Ah'm hopin' tae pick up some good breedin' stock. Ah'll wait an' see whit they're like but if they're good Ah'll take them. A short visit this time an' we'll be headin' aff as soon as we're loaded."

When Mathew went into the kitchen Elsie asked, "They didnae wait long Mathew was there summat up?"

"He jist said they were away tae see some horses."

Mathew and Elsie felt that there was something not quite right, but they would never have guessed that John was trying to keep a distance between Robert and Coralina.

On John's return to the camp Coralina did not mention the trip to Dalgarven nor did she mention Robert. Mary on the other hand had question after question.

"Who did you see? Where did you go? Did you bring back a sweetie?"

On and on the questions went to John and young Johnny until they were both tired of listening to her. She followed them around ending up at the horse field, and then much to her shock John hoisted Mary up and plunked her down on the back of Mizzie, one of the brood mares.

"Da, Da, whit ye daein' Da?"

"Jist hang on tae it's mane and sit tight on her back, she'll no' hurt ye."

Mary's face was a picture and John stole a glance at young Johnny who lowered his head to hide his grin. Although many of the girls could ride, it was the lads who usually worked and exercised them, but Mary was driving her father crazy, and he thought she would have enough to think about holding on to Mizzie. All the horses were safe around the children and Mizzie was the gentlest of them all. She had an instinct that made John feel as though she was reading his mind.

Mizzie's feathered mane was thick and long and reached the bottom of her stomach. She was mostly black with large white patches scattered over her hindquarters and shoulders. Looking at her serious face one would realise that she had two different coloured eyes, one brown and one blue. Her feathered fetlocks were thick and white in contrast to her black legs and her thick tail was white like her mane. Whenever she galloped across the field, she was a beautiful sight and John would often stand and watch her.

Mizzie's ears flickered back a little and then forward as Mary settled on to her broad back and then she slowly walked forward. Mary opened her mouth wide in a silent scream, and then suddenly she looked at her Da and started to laugh.

"Oh Da, look, Ah'm ridin' Mizzie!"

John and Johnny exchanged glances again but this time they were both surprised. They both expected Mary to be quiet, and want nothing more than to be lifted down from the horse so that she could scamper back to the camp. How wrong they were, for that was the start of Mary's passion for horses, in particular for Mizzie, and the bond was a mutual one because for some unknown reason Mizzie took a special liking to Mary too.

Mizzie was one of John's finest brood mares; she was seven years old and every second year she gave him a fine foal or filly. John remembered the day she was born and he had loved her since. She could have foaled every year, but John was happier to let her have a year to nurse her young before allowing her to mate again, in the belief that she could foal for longer rather than breeding from her every year and wearing her out.

Mary took every opportunity to run to the horse field and as soon as Mizzie saw her, she would trot to meet her with her tail held high behind her as though she was showing off. Some days if Mary was slow to arrive Mizzie would be waiting for her at the edge of the roped off field, stamping on the ground, quietly snorting her impatience. Sometimes Mary would tease Mizzie and run away from her and Mizzie would run alongside her. Mary's laughter and Mizzie's whinnying could be heard in the camp, and any that watched were sure that Mizzie was enjoying the game as much as Mary was.

One day, John watched the interaction between his youngest daughter and the horse. The top of Mary's head only came up to the middle of Mizzie's stomach, and John laughed at their antics, the pair of them running at full belt. As he watched he saw Mary adjust her pace to mimic Mizzie's canter, skipping as though she herself was a horse, when suddenly Mary reached up and grabbed Mizzie's mane. In the next moment, she was hoisting herself, half hanging upside down, before she managed to wriggle her legs and body onto Mizzie's back. Neither Mizzie nor Mary broke stride and all John could do was stand there and watch in amazement as the two behaved as one, Mizzie's long mane flying as she galloped around the field, and Mary's hair blowing back behind her. His heart almost stopped, and then, as if that wasn't bad enough, he watched Mizzie with Mary on her back leap over the rope that enclosed the horses.

"Holy Mither!" he said, as he started to run, but what he was hoping to do he did not know, and then just as quickly Mary turned Mizzie and rode back to meet her father.

"Did ye see me? Did ye see me, Da?"

Only then did John realise that young Johnny was beside him, both of them looking at Mary with a mixture of concern and amazement.

"Get aff."

One look at her father's face told Mary that he wasn't happy; in fact, he was mad at her. She swung her leg round and slipped to the ground with a sheepish look on her face.

"Whit were ye thinkin' Mary?"

"It jist happened Da."

"Yer aye the same Mary, ye jist dae things with oot a thought, ye gave me a fricht an' ye could ha' killed yer self or hurt Mizzie."

Johnny stood quietly beside them, but he was impressed, and thought that Mary was the wildest, bravest, most beautiful lassie that he had ever seen. Johnny was only eight, coming on nine, but in that moment, he knew that one day he would marry Mary Kelly.

"Away an' help yer sister, Ah dinnae ken how she puts up wi' ye."

Mary didn't argue, she just turned her head and kissed Mizzie's soft nose and then went back to the camp. The camp, of course, was buzzing with Mary's escapade, as a few of the women had seen Mary's leap over the rope and out of the field. Most kept their heads down to avoid eye contact with her as she walked back, but Mary being Mary, held her head high and didn't care what anyone thought.

Coralina was oblivious to Mary's escapade, she was busy fussing with things in the wagon, but although she loved her sister, she was despairing of having to do almost everything herself. Thoughts of Robert occupied her young mind, and she often romanticised about him as she carried out her daily tasks.

Chapter 13

The Appleby Horse fair was held every year in the first week in June. Although there were many fairs throughout the country, this one was the most popular in the travelling community. Almost the whole camp would pack up and travel to Appleby where they would buy, sell and trade and meet up with their own kind. The journey would take at least a week and at the end of the day's journey, those that were camping out would set up their benders and a campfire would be lit in the middle of the camp. Often this was a good excuse to sit around the fire, play a fiddle or accordion, sing songs, and tell stories of previous fairs. Eventually everyone would settle down to rest before another early rise the next morning.

This was something that everyone prepared for in advance; horses and dogs would be paraded around a roped off auction ring while others were negotiated for in private sales where they would barter with each other arguing over prices. Some Gypsies would have purchased rugs from Arab traders to sell on at the fair, while others would be selling galvi basins, pails, and jugs. Cartloads of goods were transported to sell at the fair. Most Gypsy women were good with their hands and they would bring their arts and crafts to sell and exchange with other women, and much showing off, socialising, and celebrating would be done.

The young lads would show off their riding skills by trotting and galloping bareback through the town then they would gather at the River Eden to cool off and wash their horses, but uppermost in their minds would be impressing their peers and the young lassies. Many a match would be made through meetings at the Appleby Horse fair.

John and his family and almost all of the camp set off for Appleby at dawn one fine morning in the last week in May. The sun had just risen and was warming the early morning dew on the grass, and there was an air of eager anticipation among the travellers. It would be seven or eight days before they would reach their destination nevertheless everyone looked forward to the excursion. Because this was such an important event in their calendar, wagons had been repainted, brasses polished until they were gleaming, and horses groomed to perfection. Of course, the journey being so long, meant that everything had to be refreshed each day before the next part of their travels, but no one minded the task and it was all part of the excitement.

Their personal appearance was important too; for the men, boots would be polished to a fine shine, though that wouldn't last once they started tramping through the field where the fair was held. The wives and mothers would steam jackets and trousers over a pan of boiling water to freshen them up and they would make sure that they had something bright and new to wear too. They preferred to use colourful fabrics bought or traded to make skirts, shawls, and scarves to wrap their hair in; everything had to be perfect.

Coralina had spent weeks making skirts for her and Mary, Coralina's was scarlet and full skirted so that it would look beautiful when she danced, and she had made a white petticoat to wear under it. When it was finished, she tried it on and did a few twirls in front of her aunt showing off her handiwork. She made the same outfit for Mary, but Mary's fabric was multi coloured in shades of blues and yellows. During daytime, they would wear their everyday clothes, but at night when the day's trading was over everyone would dress in their best, and gather together to sit and socialise, pass on messages or the latest news, tell stories, play music, or sing and dance. The lassies would be trying to impress the lads and the lads would be posturing and showing off.

As they got closer to their destination, other wagons would join the procession and locals would gather to watch the arrivals. Some would come to admire, some to stare in fascination, and others to complain, but the travelling families took it all in their stride. They knew that oftentimes those that stared or scorned would actually be the ones who would purchase their wares and services. Mary could hardly contain herself such was her excitement. Coralina was more dignified about the whole thing, nevertheless her grin made her cheeks ache. Young Johnny was travelling in his family's wagon so he was spared Mary's chatter and jostling about.

"For Heaven's sake Mary, have ye worms can ye no' sit still?"

"Da, Ah'm fair excited."

"Jist calm doon, and sit quiet like yer sister."

"Can Ah ride Mizzie along the street wi' the lads."

At that comment, Coralina turned and stared at Mary's audacity, and John did the same. Coralina dropped her eyes quickly, but John stared at Mary, and she knew by the look he gave her that this question should not have been asked. She so wanted to ride out with the lads, and she was too young to realise that this was inappropriate.

"Ye'll sit in the wee cart wi' me an' yer sister, an' that's as near as ye'll get to ridin' wi' the lads."

Mary turned and pulled a face at Coralina but Coralina just ignored her. When they had set up in the field, that would be their base for the duration of the fair, they would assemble little carts from parts that were stored under the wagons. There were large carts used for transporting things that would be needed by the travellers, and those that didn't have enough room to store their small carts could borrow a space in another's cart.

John had plenty of room under his wagon to carry his own cart and he was busy assembling it with Mary looking on watching his every move. Some of her attention was given in the hope that she could get back into her father's good books, but being the tomboy that she was, she was watching, because in her mind, one day, she would be building her own cart to ride through the streets with the lads. She wouldn't be doing that anytime soon, but she was about to do something that would draw everyone's attention, and that people would talk about for years to come.

While John was assembling his cart Coralina was grooming the horse that would pull it along, making it look smart, and it was as though this horse, King, knew that within a few moments he would be clipping along showing off as did everyone else during this parade through the town. Coralina had brushed his mane and tail and had fastened bells to the halter and reins. As soon as the cart was ready and John had hitched up King, he and the girls climbed on to the wooden frame that supported a narrow bench for them to sit on. It was all about showing off how you could handle a horse and cart and not so much about the cart.

"Noo' mind keep yer skirts tucked in and yer feet away fae the sides."

Coralina demurely settled herself, but Mary as always had an answer, "Aye Da, Ah hear ye, Ah'm bein' careful."

The sound of the horses' hooves could be heard clip clopping through the town as Gypsy travellers and locals alike watched. The atmosphere was electric, and everyone was happy and smiling as the riders in the parade made their way to the river Eden. The lads were out, as usual, riding bareback through the streets, some of them taking chances with their antics, and many a gasp could be heard as they passed within inches of carts or spectators. When they reached the river, those on horseback would ride right into the water to cool their horses, and of course, to show off their horsemanship. Some of the cart riders would unhitch their horses and walk down to the river to cool their beasts and let them drink after the thirsty ride; others would stand around chatting, catching up on the latest news or gossip.

Chapter 14

Mary stood and stared in fascination at some Shire Horses that were in the roped off area with Vanners and other workhorses. The Shires towered above the others and Mary watched as some horses were led around the ring and others stood quietly by their owners. Buyers wandered freely among them, looking, nodding to the owners, sometimes drawing a hand down a horse leg, or across their back. Some examined a horse's teeth and this was a sure sign that they were interested in buying. Mary began to make her way around the ring so that she could get a closer look at them.

"Mister, can Ah stroke yer horse?" said Mary. The man she spoke to looked down at her, hardly interested, but nodding his approval. Mary went under the rope and up to the giant of a horse and reached up to stroke its belly. The owner of the horse was chatting to another man and they both glanced at Mary and laughed at her.

"Whit's his name?"

The owner looked down at Mary once more, "Sam," he said indifferently. Mary wandered round Sam stroking the parts that she could reach, her neck straining as she looked up admiring the horse and talking to him.

"Aye yer a grand lad Sam, yer a giant, big strong legs, aye yer beautiful." Sam was listening to Mary but not reacting very much to her compliments. The two men had another quick glance at Mary and laughed at her while carrying on with their conversation.

"Can Ah ride him?" Mary asked,

Both men bellowed with laughter, more intent on doing a bit of business than tolerating a silly wee lassie. "Aye, if ye can get yer self up ye can ride him," he replied laughing with the other man.

Mary turned and walked away, and as far as the two men were concerned that was the end of the matter, but it wasn't the end of the matter to Mary. She made her way around the stallholders and noticed that one woman had a display of early carrots, "Missus, can Ah get a carrot?"

"Away ya' cheeky lass."

"Ah have a coin."

"Ah'll take' yer coin then," the woman said, and handed Mary a couple of carrots.

Mary grabbed the carrots, and ran off back to the horse ring, ducking and diving around people as she made her way back to the Shire horse. The two men were still chatting as Mary approached the Shire. She walked around and stood in front of the huge horse that paid her no mind. Mary took a carrot from her pocket, and letting the horse see it, she bit off a piece, and made exaggerated noises of pleasure as she crunched it. Sam's ears flicked forward in interest and looking down at Mary, he sniffed and snorted at her hair. Mary bit another piece of carrot and palm opened she offered it to Sam. It was gone in a second leaving a large area of moisture on Mary's hand; the Shire was more interested now. Mary giggled as she took a step back and Sam took a step forward. Another piece of carrot was bitten off, offered, and accepted.

The owner and his colleague were half watching and half ignoring Mary, assuming that all she was doing was giving titbits to the Shire. They were only remotely interested in her presence and continued chatting. Mary offered Sam another small piece of carrot, which was eagerly received. She bit another piece of carrot and placed it on the ground between her and Sam. The Shire lowered his head to the ground and snaffled up the carrot. Mary took another step back and once more placed a piece of carrot on the ground between herself and the horse. This time, when the horse stretched down to get the carrot Mary ruffled his mane. She took another step back, broke off another piece, placed it on the ground, and stepped to the side. As she expected the big Shire lowered its head to the ground and without another thought, Mary leaned in, grabbed a handful of mane with both hands, and held on for dear life as the Shire lifted its head and Mary with it. In the next moment, Mary was sitting on the horse's neck, giggling and clinging on for dear life, and then she just wiggled down his neck, onto his back, leaning forward rubbing his face, and telling him how clever he was. Then she sat there proudly looking down at the owner and his companion, who were both standing with their mouths hanging open at her antics, her audacity, and her ingenuity.

"What the devil?" said the owner.

"Did ye see that wee lassie, did ye see whit she jist did?"

"Ah'm fair flummert," was the reply.

"Whose lassie is that?"

"Ah dinnae ken, she's wan o' oors, but Ah've nae idea whit family."

"Ye said if Ah could get up, Ah could ride him, Ah'm up," said Mary confidently, and as the men, and others who had seen Mary's bold move watched; Sam showing off, proudly walked forward and began to circle the horse ring.

Across the field, Coralina was standing by her Da and young Johnny as they chatted with other travellers. There was much for her to see and take in but she became aware of a hubbub of conversation as though something different was happening, and as she diverted her gaze to the source, her mouth fell open. "Da! Da! Its Mary." Her father turned and anxiously looked at Coralina, because he could tell by her voice that there was something not quite right. He started to scan the crowds around him leaning to the left and the right to see if he could see Mary between the folk that were milling about.

"Da! Da! Look!" she said, and pointed to the other side of the ring; and there was his Mary, visible above the crowds, sitting on top of the big Shire horse grinning from ear to ear.

"Holy Mither, that lassie'll be the death o' me." He ran towards the ring, stooped under the rope, and ran between other horses and up to where Mary was. Coralina and Johnny were at his heels when he reached her.

"Get aff!"

"But Da!"

He reached up, grabbed Mary from the horse, and glowered at the owner. "Did you put ma lass up there?" he asked angrily, standing, fists clenched, and ready for a fight.

"Here noo, haud yer horses, yer lassie did it hersel'."

"Dinnae be ridiculous man, she can barely reach its belly."

"Aye, an' that's whit Ah thought when Ah told her she could ride it if she could get on him hersel'. She's a wide wan that yin. Next thing she's conned the big fella tae put his heed doon an' she climbs up his neck. Ah've never seen onythin' like it! Ah recognise ye. You'll be John Kelly then, Ah've seen ye aboot. Ah was awfy sorry tae hear aboot ye losin' yer wife." He stuck out his hand to shake John's.

"Aye, that's me and this vixen is Mary, and she'll feel ma anger on her backside."

"Aye well, she's your lass, but that was a clever thing she did, she has a knack wi' the horses. Whit age is she?"

"She's nearly eight goin' on eighty an' Ah cannae keep up wi' her."

The owner of the Shire and his friend regaled John about Mary's antics and her determination to ride the big horse. While they were speaking, someone sounded a bell announcing the auction was about to start so John shook hands with the two men and holding on to Mary he made his way around to watch the bidding.

The auction was a favourite with all the fair goers as this was where you could see the antics of the bidders; some would merely raise an eyebrow to indicate a bid while others, remaining perfectly still, would simply move their index finger and the eagle eyed auctioneer would spot that and up the price would go. Others yet would wink or nod but the auctioneer didn't miss a trick. When a horse was sold the seller and the buyer would meet outside the ring behind the auctioneer and exchange pleasantries and as the custom would have it, the seller would give a penny to the buyer 'for luck'. It was the height of bad manners not to offer that lucky penny and some would say that if you didn't then you might never sell another thing.

Later in the evening, when they were sitting around the fires it became apparent that the entire fair knew about Mary's antics, and Mary, well she was delighted to be the centre of attention, but John wasn't happy, and Coralina was disgusted with her sister.

Chapter 15

As Mary became more outgoing, Coralina became more reserved and quiet. She continued to love and care for her little sister, she took care of the wagon, and looked after her father's needs, but she was withdrawn and often looked sad. The Mither and Isabella noticed this too, and often asked Coralina what was wrong with her, but she just stated that she was fine and that there was nothing wrong. Mary was so wrapped up in herself that initially she didn't notice the changes in her big sister, but as the winter came, she realised that her sister was ailing for something. Her instincts had been dormant largely because she was more interested in what she wanted rather than what was going on around her.

She began to watch Coralina, and as she watched, she became filled with a sense of sadness so deep that it was painful. Coralina's sadness was hidden so well that Mary found it hard to read the reason for it, and suddenly, looking at her sister that she loved so dearly, silent tears began to roll down her cheeks. Coralina was engrossed in what she was doing, but when she glanced at her sister and saw her tears, she jumped up and went to her side. Putting her arm around Mary's shoulder she asked, "Mary! Whit's up wi' ye?"

"Ah'm sad for ye Coralina. Ah can feel yer hurtin' an' Ah dinnae ken whit tae dae or why yer hurtin so bad."

"Ah'm jist sad Mary, an' Ah dinnae ken why, but dinnae say onythin' tae ma Da or Auntie Isabella or the Mither. Ah'm jist sad that's a'." As the words were coming out of her mouth Coralina had the merest thought of Robert, and at the same time Mary sensed the thought and she gasped.

"Yer thinkin' o' Robert Miller!"

Coralina's face reddened, "Naw, wheesht, yer' wrang."

"Ah'm no' wrang, Ah know yer thinkin' o' him."

"Please Mary, ye'll get me in tae trouble fae Da an' Auntie Isabella, she tell't me tae stay away fae Gorja's an' Ah huvnae seen him, but Ah think o' him a' the time." Coralina was crying now and Mary put her arms around her.

"Ah'm a big lassie noo an Ah ken whit it feels like tae love a lad, Ah love Johnny an' Ah would be fair upset if Ah couldnae see him. Ah'll no' say a word Coralina."

Coralina laughed at her sister through her tears, and then the two girls embraced and cried quietly together, but from that day Mary paid more attention to her sister and tried to be more helpful. As Mary tuned in to her sister she was also tuning into other energies around her, and she began to develop an understanding of her gift. She realised that just by watching someone, just by being in the moment, she could read a person's emotions, and more often than not, she could predict things about them.

That was a long cold winter for everyone, and temperatures were below freezing so keeping warm was a priority for the travellers. John was thankful that he had chosen the wooden wagon with the wood burning stove, which kept the girls warm and cosy. Fetching water from the river meant breaking the ice to access the freezing cold water below. The full pail was carried back to the campfire and decanted into the big galvi milk churns that were used to store the water. These sat near the fire to prevent the water from freezing.

Their over winter supplies were running low, and poaching was the only way to put food on the table. Those who didn't have a stove that they could light or share would huddle in their wagons, their shoulders draped in blankets with only the heat from Tilly lamps to keep them warm, but in such small spaces the heat soon built up and kept them cosy. That was the year that the old Mither died. She just passed away in her sleep. Mary sensed it first, and ran to her aunt's wagon. "Auntie Isabella Ah think summat's wrang wi' the Mither."

Isabella ran across to her mother-in-law's wagon, but Mary hung back afraid to go any further. At first, Isabella thought she was only in a deep sleep, but as she approached, she became more concerned. She looked at the Mither and she could see that her skin was smooth and free of the lines that normally creased her face. She reached out and touched the Mither's face and it was ice cold. She drew back suddenly as she realised that her mother-in-law was gone. She stood there with her hands covering her mouth as grief poured through her and she thought of her husband George. She tried to think of how she would tell him that his mother had passed over. She didn't know that young Mary had gone to fetch him, and just as she was fretting over how to break the news, George appeared in the wagon behind her. No words were necessary, they just stared in shock at each other, and then Isabella moved to one side to allow George space to approach his mother. He knelt by her narrow bed and took one of her cold hands in his. He whispered silently, "Aw Mam, Mam, whit are wi' tae dae with oot ye?" Isabella watched sadly, as tears wet her husband's face, mirroring her own.

After some time, he stood and turned towards Isabella, took both her hands in his, lowered his head and put his lips to her hands.

"Mither," he said, and Isabella gasped as she realised that she was now the oldest in the camp, and the responsibility of advising, and overseeing discipline, praise and decision making was now hers. This was a daunting thought, and she didn't feel as though she had the knowledge, skills, or experience to fill this role as the Mither of the camp. She was wrong; every day in the presence of the Mither had been a lesson for her, and the Mither had taught her well, nevertheless, she was afraid of what might lie ahead for her.

Isabella and George spent some time quietly grieving and saying silent prayers. By the time they were ready to leave the wagon, everyone in the camp had gathered outside in the cold chill air. George emerged first, and as he appeared on the steps, he stood for a moment and surveyed his fellow travellers, his family, and his friends. All of them, affected by the same sadness, gazed upon him, and as he made his way down the wooden steps from the wagon, each in turn shook his hand, embraced him, and offered words of support.

Isabella had known this would happen, and allowed a little time for these sympathies to be offered before she too left the wagon. Her heart was pounding in her chest as she stood at the threshold of the wagon. One by one, each of the gathering approached her, took her hand, and said, "Mither," to show their respect to her.

They gathered around the fire, sitting up through the following nights, talking about Mither Morrison, sharing memories of things that she had said or done, speaking of how she had praised, chastised, or helped them. They all had memories to share and held several wakes, until it was time for her to be laid to rest at Janefield Cemetery.

The day after the funeral, a sad procession took her wagon, with all her possessions intact, away from the camp to a secluded area, and set fire to it. As they watched the wagon and its contents burn, they grieved for a life lived, and a loved one gone.

Chapter 16

The first signs of spring were beginning to show and that cold, cold, feeling was disappearing. With each passing day, the nights grew shorter and the days grew longer. Snowdrops peeping through the still hard ground delighted everyone who saw them, and spirits began to rise. Now that spring was on the way, they could begin to focus on their plans and tasks to earn a living for the year ahead.

Isabella had been keeping a close eye on Coralina, aware that she had become withdrawn and unhappy, though true to her nature, she never complained. George was preparing to go on the road with his tools, for his skills shoeing horses and sharpening tools would be in great demand around the local farms. John would be making his trip around the Ayrshire farms, where he would negotiate the purchase or sale of horses, and on his journey, he would replenish the stocks of flour, oats, and pulses for himself and the rest of the camp, finishing up as usual at Dalgarven Mill.

Isabella had fretted over Coralina, and she came to the realisation that it was her place to do something about her. She knew John would be at the horse field so she made her way over to find him.

"A word in yer ear John."

"Aye, whit's up Isabella?" he said to his sister in law, straightening up from cleaning the hoof of one of the horses.

"Ah'm fair worried aboot Coralina."

John sighed and shook his head, "Aye, me an' a' she's been awfy quiet, an' even if Ah ask her whit's up, she tells me nowt."

"Well John, she's no' been away fae the camp for a good long while, maybe ye should think aboot takin' her wi' ye this time."

"Whit aboot Robert Miller?"

"She's a sensible lass, an' fae whit ye say about the Millers they're a guid family, jist keep yer eye on her."

"Ah'll see, Ah'll think aboot it, away wi' ye Mither, Ah have a lot tae dae for the morrow," he said, laughing at giving her a formal title. Isabella smiled to herself as she made her way back to her wagon and she felt as though she had achieved something, little as it was.

When John was finished all he had to do to prepare for his trip, he made his way back to his wagon to find Coralina sitting crocheting small cotton doilies that she would trim with fancy coloured beads or shells to sell around the villages in the summer time.

"Whit ye daein' lass?"

"Makin' doilies Da."

"Ye must have a fair few noo Coralina."

"Aye Da, Ah've aboot twenty."

"Ah'm thinkin, if ye could tear yer self away fae yer crochetin', maybe ye would like tae come on the road wi' me the morrow, might happen that ye could sell some doilies tae?"

Coralina sat quietly, for a few moments, she didn't lift her head, afraid to show her excitement, and then, "Aye Da, that would be nice."

John had expected more of a reaction, but he was pleased that Coralina didn't seem overly bothered. "Aye well, get any stuff ye need ready for yer self an' yer sister, an' we'll be off early mornin'."

Mary was in the horse field with Mizzie, and although Coralina was desperate to share the news, she decided to wait until Mary came back to the wagon. She didn't have long to wait, for a short while later Mary came running in bursting full of excitement, having just been told by her Da that they were both going on the trip.

"Coralina, have ye heard? Did Da tell ye he's lettin' us go wi' him an' Johnny the morrow? Ye'll be able tae see Robert."

"Mary wheesht, dinnae mention his name, ma Da'll no' let us go if he hears ye. Get yer stuff ready."

"Are ye no' pleased Coralina?"

"Aye, Ah'm pleased, Ah jist didnae want to be too keen. Away, get yer stuff ready."

Coralina checked on the things that they would need to take with them for the trip, and Mary, while chatting ten to the dozen, busied herself hindering rather than helping. Coralina wasn't listening to any of Mary's chatter. Her mind was on the trip to Dalgarven and seeing Robert again. As with any budding romance, she was filled with fears and her thoughts were racing.

'*Did he like her as much as she liked him? What if he had a lassie? Maybe it would be better if she didn't go with her Da.* She wanted to see him so badly that she was willing to take the chance.

The Sun had just risen when they set off from Glasgow Green that Monday morning; the March air was clear, but although it was still cold there were signs of spring everywhere. They would travel towards Shawlands passing the grand Pollok Estate, on towards Barrhead, and then by the Crofthead Mill in Neilston. Occasionally they could pick up threads and fabric samples from the mill that the women would use for making new clothes, or repairing old ones. They would save scraps of cloth and remnants for crafts, and then sell these crafts around the villages or at the fairs. After their visit to the mill, they would head along Lochlibo Road, on through Shillford ending that part of the journey at Lugton, a small hamlet in East Renfrewshire, where they would set up camp by Lugton water.

Once the family and the horses were tended to and settled, John would saddle up one of the horses and ride up to West Halket Farm taking a couple of young horses he had brought with him. He had promised them to the farmer, one for him, and another for his neighbour. Later, when the business was done John would walk from the campsite to the Lugton Inn and have a welcome pint of beer, knowing that Coralina would be mindful of Mary and Johnny, and the horses tethered nearby. The landlord at the Inn was always pleased to see him and often gave him a loaf of fresh bread to take away with him.

The next day after an early start they would head for a dairy farm in Dunlop where they would pick up cheeses for the camp. By lunchtime, the party would be feasting on lovely chunks of fresh bought cheese and the crusty bread from the Inn. Everyone was enjoying the trip but none more so than Coralina. With each part of the journey, her excitement grew, although she did her best not to appear too eager, for fear of her father realising that Robert Miller was the source of her enthusiasm.

The last horse was to be delivered to Auchintiber, and after the business was done there it was on through Kilwinning, and finally to Dalgarven. Coralina's stomach was in knots by the time they reached the outskirts of Kilwinning because before long they were turning into the mill yard.

Chapter 17

Robert heard their wagon before he saw it; it could have been anyone coming for flour, but the hitch in his stomach was the sign that he was hoping that it would be John Kelly, and that he would have brought Coralina with him. As the wagon came into view, he was torn between running to it, or standing his ground. He was going on eighteen now, and in Coralina's absence he had filled out considerably. His boyish good looks had developed, and anyone could see that he would soon be a strong handsome man.

Coralina was blushing as she looked at him and smiled coyly. Mary was grinning like a Cheshire cat, and she sneaked a look at her sister who glowered back at her. Young Johnny was the first to jump from the cart,

"Are ye a' right Robert," he said, and Robert acknowledged with a grin and a nod.

"Guid tae see ye Mister Kelly, have ye had a guid journey?"

"Aye Robert, Ah have that, how's the family?"

"They're both good, Ma's in the kitchen an' Da's in the mill. Ah'll tell them yer here," and with a quick glance at Coralina, he turned and walked off to let his parents know that the John Kelly had arrived.

Robert could hardly see in front of him, all he could see was Coralina's face. "*My Lord! She's mair lovely than Ah remembered, Ah'll be heartbroken if she has a fella,*" he thought. He stuck his head around the back door of the farmhouse, "Mam, the Kelly's are here, Ah'm jist away tae shout ma Da." He knew that they were climbing down from the wagon but he didn't dare turn and look, so he carried on to the mill and called his father. "That's the Kelly's here Da." He tried to remain calm and casual as he walked back round to where they were waiting.

"Hello Robert," said Mary, skipping up towards him.

He ruffled her hair, "My, ye've grown a fair bit Mary," and to Johnny he said, "Is this lassie still givin' ye grief?" He was still laughing as he glanced over to Coralina, "Coralina," he nodded at her, "are ye well?"

"Ah am Robert, yer self?"

"Aye, ye'll be ready for a cuppa."

Just at that moment, Elsie and Mathew arrived at the wagon and shook hands with John before leading them all into the kitchen.

"Yer in luck the day John, Ah've jist taken some soda scones aff the griddle; come away in an' sit at the table."

After they had eaten and enthused over Elsie's home baking, John, Elsie, and Mathew sat and chatted while the others went off outside, and while Mary and Johnny amused themselves exploring, Robert and Coralina found time to chat. They walked over to the mill and sat on the mill wall above the stream.

"Ah've' missed ye Coralina."

"Aye, Ah've missed ye tae Robert, though Ah was worried ye widnae' remember me, it's been a fair while, an' Ah thought ye would have plenty tae think aboot."

"Never a day passed when Ah didnae think of ye Coralina."

"Ah'm glad tae hear that Robert, Ah thought aboot ye a' the time. Ah thought ye might have taken a wife?"

"There's only wan lass for me Coralina, an' here she is afore me."

"Oh Robert, ye cannae talk like that! Ma Da would have the skin aff yer back if he thought ye were sayin' such things."

"Yer Da likes me."

"Aye, an' he likes yer family tae, but Ah have tae marry fae ma ane kind, it's expected, an' if Ah dinnae marry a Gypsy lad it would bring shame on me an' ma family."

"Dae ye love me Coralina? That's a' that matters, dae ye love me?"

Coralina had been going to Dalgarven since she was a toddler and she and Robert had played together and run about the fields since they were small. She knew in her heart that there would be no other for her.

"Aye Robert, Ah think Ah have aye loved ye."

"Well Ah'll speak tae yer Da."

"Ye cannae Robert, if ye speak tae ma Da ye'll never see me again, 'cause he'll no' allow it. He'll no' let me come wi' him ever again."

Coralina was silent, crying now, and Robert felt sick to his stomach.

"Dinnae worry then lass, Ah'll no' say a word but Ah'll make a plan. Will ye come away wi' me?"

"They'll come after us; the whole camp will come lookin."

"Ah'll take care o' ye Coralina, they'll no' find us. Just keep things as they are an' dinnae say a word, jist give me yer promise that ye will be ma wife."

"Ah will Robert, Ah promise."

"Ma Da has been guid tae me an' gave me a wage every week for helpin him, so Ah've money put by, enough tae gie us a guid start; we'll jist run aff and get wed, an' that will be that. Dae ye think yer Da will be at the fair in Neilston in July?"

"Aye, 'cause he'll be looking tae show some horses an' pick up some new stock."

"Ah'll make a plan, if he brings ye tae any o' the fairs be ready tae go an' that will be that. If he disnae, well jist be ready whenever he brings you, whether it be here or a fair, an' Ah'll be waitin' an' ready tae go."

"Ah'll be ready Robert, Ah love ye Robert, but Ah better get back; Ah'll see ye in a bit."

Robert went for a walk by the river Garnock. He sat on the sand bed at the edge of the river and stared out in front of him. He had thought that he would spend his whole life here and take over the tenancy of the mill from his father. His mind drifted…Dalgarven was his home, and it had everything that a man could want to set up a home and a family. The mill was at the centre of the community, no doubt, it was hard work providing flour and oatmeal for the village and the surrounding areas, but he loved it. It was a bustling village, where everyone knew everyone else, and they did not have to travel elsewhere for tradesmen, as they were all there within this small community of around thirty or so houses; slaters, saddlers, carpenters or joiners lived and worked within a short distance. The local sawmill supplied wood for building, and the women could find cloth for their clothing or other needs.

He thought back to when he was just three years old; there was shouting and screaming in the early hours of the morning, his father grabbing him from his sleep and running into the yard with his mother. It was absolute pandemonium; the mill was on fire, and the fire had already spread to some of the surrounding buildings. His father thrust him into his mother's arms; she was crying and screaming, and holding him so close that he could hardly turn his head to see what was happening. The barns and byres had caught alight, and his father was in the middle of the melee of villagers trying to save livestock and their homes. He would never forget that day, or the days, weeks and months that followed, when everyone worked together and rebuilt all that was damaged, or destroyed by the fire.

As a small child, he was unable to do much to help, but he watched and learned from his father and others. As he grew, he developed a keen interest in fixing and building things. Now as an adult he could turn his hand to anything; he understood the engineering mechanisms of the mill machinery and could carry out repairs if necessary, he could work with wood, patching or building as required, and he was confident around livestock.

'Surely,' he thought, *'Ah kin find any kind o' work; Ah kin turn ma hand tae anything'.*

He sighed a deep heart-wrenching sigh; he loved his village, his home, but he would overcome any obstacle or face any challenge if it meant Coralina would be his wife.

Chapter 18

Coralina and her family left early the next morning to begin the long journey home, and it was with a heavy heart that Robert watched the love of his life leaving in the cart laden with flour and other supplies.

"He has feelin's for that lass," said Elsie Miller to her husband.

"Aye, Ah think yer right, but he keeps them under wraps."

"It's jist as well, for nothin can come of it."

"Dinnae worry, he'll find a lass soon enough, and then ye'll be nursin' gran' weans," laughed Mathew as he put his arm over her shoulder and led her back to the kitchen.

Robert stood there, watching until the cart was out of sight, and then he took himself into the mill back to work while he thought and planned. The Neilston Fair occurred in the first week of July, he counted out the time in his mind; he had about four months to get ready, but he still had to think about how they would manage this daring escape and where they could go so that no one would find them.

Robert had his own horse and cart that he used to deliver supplies from the mill to anyone that couldn't manage to come for them. His father had helped him to build it the year before and Robert had taken his time about planning the size and style, it was six feet long at the back with deep sides and a storage box under the seat. The box was big enough to carry tools to fix a wheel or help another out while making deliveries. When it was time to leave' he would stow some blankets in the box, along with the canopy that covered the cart when the weather was bad.

He would carry a small amount of feed for the horses; mostly they would be able to graze when they stopped for a rest. As far as their needs went, he had enough money to buy their provisions. There was no knowing how long it would be until they found somewhere safe to settle, so he would be careful with what money he had.

Where to go was the biggest problem that he had to solve. *"Perhaps it should be somewhere fairly remote, but somewhere that Ah could find work, but maybe a town would be better."* He pondered on this for a while thinking that the first place the Gypsies would look for them would be the mills scattered around the country, but he would do anything, any job, as long as they could be together.

Coralina was just as quiet on the journey home as she had been before they set off, and John began to think it was just because she was growing up and changing. She and her sister were pretty girls, but now Coralina was becoming a beautiful young woman. Her skin was fresh with a golden glow, and her long, wavy black hair framed her face as it tumbled down over her shoulders. John was sure that once she had found someone to love, that would love her equally in return, she would be happy. He began to think of the lads that he knew that were around her age, and he decided that he would do something about finding her a match at the Appleby Fair.

Coralina would have been horrified if she could have read her father's mind, but her mind was racing with other possibilities. She had taken all the lace doilies that she had made, and each time they stopped, she offered them for sale to whoever was around. She sold them all; she had been doing this for several years and her father always made her keep her pennies.

'For yer bottom drawer Coralina,' he would say to her when she offered him her earnings as she always did.

Occasionally she would sort her farthings, ha'pennies, and pennies, and her Da would change her coppers for a bright silver shilling. In those days, a shilling was a lot of money, the average weekly wage being around ten shillings. Coralina had already amassed a small fortune of five pounds and four shillings and this was safely stowed away in her bottom drawer. She decided there and then, that on her return to the camp, she would set aside the four shillings plus the odd coppers that she had earned on the journey. She would give this money to her sister to give her a start with her dowry. Mary would soon have to start thinking about making things to sell so that she too could save for her wedding day. So far, Mary had shown no interest in making things with her hands, preferring to be in the horse field, riding Mizzie, and helping with the other horses. Small though she was, she would carry water, feed, or straw and take on any task that Johnny did, almost as though she was out to keep up with him at least, or at best, better him. Coralina knew that when she left Mary would have little time for indulging in her preferences.

When they finally arrived back at the camp, everyone came out to collect the provisions that John had brought back with him. Money changed hands, and as was the tradition, there was always an extra penny given *'for luck'*. The horses were unhitched and led to the field to graze and then the cart was cleaned, the wheels were oiled and it was stowed away for future use. When everything was back in order, John went across to have a cup of tea and a chat with Isabella. "Well Isabella, Ah dinnae think the trip did much for Coralina's mood. She still seems ower quiet tae me. Ah'm thinking that it's high time she was wed, an' Ah'm thinking Ah should have a chat wi' ma cousins at Appleby Fair'; whit dae ye think o' that?" he said, nursing his cup.

They were outdoors sitting on wooden boxes set by the fire.

"Aye ye might be right John, have ye anybody in mind?"

"Aye, there's wan or two come tae mind but she's never shown any interest in them."

"She's been too busy mindin' Mary, John, that's half the problem."

"Aye, ye could be right. It's by time Ah had another word wi' Mary, she needs tae gie' her sister a break an' help her."

John and Isabella sat there, sipping their tea and musing over Coralina's future and a potential match for her.

"Have ye said onythin' tae Coralina aboot this John?"

"Nah', no' yet."

Neither of them had noticed Mary, who had been sitting quietly on the grass nearby, nor did they realise that she had heard them. Mary slipped away, her mind racing. She couldn't wait to tell Coralina what she had heard.

Chapter 19

Coralina was kneeling on the floor of the wagon going through her things; in her mind, she was planning what she could to take with her, and how she could hide things from her father. Her dowry money was the first thing she looked at, and then she looked for a box that she could use to put the spare shillings and change into for Mary's start. She was doing that when Mary appeared.

"Come wi' me Coralina?"

"Whit for?"

"Jist come wi' me."

"Ah'm busy Mary, Ah've things tae dae."

"Jist listen tae me, ye need tae come wi' me the noo. Ah need tae tell ye summat."

Coralina stood up and followed Mary, "Whit is it?"

"Wheesht, jist come wi' me."

Coralina followed Mary out of the camp until they were well away from anyone that could overhear them.

"Ah have summat tae tell ye."

"Spit it oot then."

"Ma Da is plannin' tae merry ye aff at the Appleby Fair!"

"Whit dae ye mean?"

"Ah heard him talkin' tae Mither Isabella, an' he was sayin' that come the fair at Appleby he was gonnae talk tae the cousins for a fella for ye tae wed!"

"Never! Ye must be mistaken'."

"Ah'm tellin ye, it's because ye have been quiet, they think ye need tae be wed an' startin' a family."

Coralina put her head in her hands and the tears began to flow. "He cannae dae that, he cannae dae that!"

"Ye'll no' have ony choice Coralina, if ma Da says yer getting merried then yer getting merried an' that will be a' there is tae it."

Coralina knew for sure now that she had to make every effort to get away before the Appleby Fair, and she prayed that her Da would take them to the Neilston fair. She couldn't think what she would do if he decided not to take her.

"Whit are ye gonnae dae Coralina? Ah think Robert loves ye."

Filled with the romance of the idea, Mary surprised Coralina by announcing, "Could ye no' run away an' merry Robert?"

"Mary wheesht! Ye'll get us in trouble if ye say that."

"Heavens above," Coralina thought to herself, *"does she ken everythin'?"*

Mary jumped back, realisation dawning on her, "Yer' gonnae run away wi' Robert!"

Coralina leapt at Mary, and grabbed her by her shoulders and shook her hard. Mary was shocked, Coralina had never shown her any anger, and had never laid a hand on her.

"Ah'm warnin' ye Mary, dinnae ever talk like that again."

Both girls were crying now, Mary because Coralina was so scared and angry, and Coralina because she was afraid that Mary might slip up and the secret would be out.

"Ah promise ye Coralina, Ah'll never say a word, Ah promise. Will ye tell me afore ye go?"

Both girls had tears streaming down their faces. Coralina held her little sister in a tight embrace, "Ah'm no' goin' onywhere the noo Mary, an' if Ah am ye'll be the first tae know."

The girls washed their faces in the river, and for a while, they walked quietly, each with their own thoughts occupying their minds. Mary began to think about what her life would be like without her big sister. She began to realise that what, for a moment, had seemed like an exciting thought, would mean that she might never see her big sister again. Coralina already understood that eventuality, and the thought of leaving her family was breaking her heart, but she knew that it was the only way.

Over the next few weeks, both girls busied themselves. Coralina tried to act as normal, but every waking thought was focused on preparing for her departure and thinking about the Neilston Fair and what she would have to take with her. Subtly, she tried to point out to her sister the things that she did on a daily basis. Neither acknowledged the reasoning behind this, but Mary understood, and played her part in listening and not saying a word about the imminent event.

"Whit's wrang wi' these lassies Isabella?" John asked.

"They're jist settlin' doon John, they're growin', ye should be proud o' them."

"Aye', Ah' am, but they're awfy quiet an' they're aye whisperin' tae each other."

Isabella laughed, "Ye should be glad aboot that John, Mary's getting a big lassie an' she's takin' her share. Coralina has been a guid mither tae her."

"Aye, happens ye might be right."

"Ye'll see a change in them when it's time tae go tae the fair they'll start tae get excited then an' ye'll no' get a minute's peace."

However, that wouldn't be the case, because when it came time to go to the fair, both girls would be aware that this could be the last days that they would see each other. John was preoccupied preparing the horses so he didn't pay much attention to the girls, and just let them get on with what they were doing. From time to time Mary helped her father and Johnny with the grooming, and Johnny noticed how quiet she was. He was reluctant to say anything, but he watched her, and he watched the subtleties between her and Coralina. He wondered to himself what was different, or more to the point, what had happened to make things different between them. Coralina had always been the more serious of the two, and Mary was always 'happy go lucky', but she had become more like her sister over the past few weeks. He often saw the girls deep in conversation and wondered about them.

All too soon, it was time to go to the Neilston Fair. Coralina was sick to her stomach and Mary was much the same. The girls climbed into the cart with Johnny at the front in charge of the reins, while John rode behind leading his horses. The sisters sat in the back of the cart whispering to each other, "Whit's gonnae happen Coralina?"

"Ah dinnae ken, Ah'll jist watch for Robert an' see whit happens."

"Are ye scared?"

"Aye."

"Ah'm scared tae."

"Ah've left summat under ma blanket for ye, for yer bottom drawer tae gie ye a start. Ye need tae think aboot makin' some money."

"Dinnae worry aboot that, Ah'll tell fortunes an' get a sixpence for that, but no' the noo, Ah'm too wee, next year maybe, an' Johnny'll look after me."

Coralina nodded, she knew Mary would be able to do that, and she would probably make good money.

Chapter 20

Before long they had reached Neilston and made their way along the road, busy with carts and wagons, carriages and pedestrians, and folks leading or riding horses. Coralina was agitated and Mary was clutching her hand, thankfully, John who was riding King, was too busy leading his sale horses, and nodding to familiar faces to notice how the girls were. Johnny, leading the cart, turned into the fairground, and began to head for the spot that they usually camped in when Mary whispered, "Ah can see him Coralina, OUCH!" she shouted as Coralina gripped her hand tightly.

"Aye, so can Ah."

Once Johnny had halted the cart, John led the horses to the roped off area where he would tie them loosely and let them settle down.

Robert approached the cart, "Hello there Johnny, Ah thought Ah might see ye here the day, are ye well?"

"Aye Robert, are the family wi' ye?"

"Nah, it's jist me the day." As Johnny jumped down from the cart and tended to the lead horse Robert went to the back of the cart and whispered to Coralina, "Ah'll be waitin' at the gate wi' ma cart, come as soon as ye can an' be ready to go." In a louder voice, "Hello there Mary."

With her eyes wide with apprehension, dreading what was about to happen, Mary looked at him and nodded, "Robert."

Robert made his way towards his cart, hitched near the gate and jumped onto it. He waited until there was a space between those coming in then he directed his horse out onto the street to wait for Coralina.

"Johnny, tell ma Da that Coralina an' me are jist away for a look an' we'll be back in a wee while," said Mary, and then she held out her hand to Coralina and said, "Are ye comin' then." Without a word, Coralina took the bag that she had stowed in the cart earlier. Hand in hand, they made their way through the crowds. Coralina had tears running down her face and when she looked at Mary, she saw that her eyes had filled too. It seemed as though Mary was taking charge, and Coralina knew in her heart that Mary would be fine without her, but the more she thought about leaving her little sister the more the ache in her heart grew.

"Hurry up Coralina," said Mary, as she tugged, almost dragged, her sister between the crowds that were building up. Then suddenly, before Coralina had any more time to think about what she was doing, they reached the gate, and there was Robert, waiting outside the field, anxiously watching for them.

"Go! Go quick! Afore anyone notices, Ah'll aye love ye an' Ah'll think o' ye every day. Send word if ye can, go now hurry."

Coralina couldn't speak for the lump in her throat. Robert jumped down from his cart. "Come tae the back o' the cart, pretend yer reachin' for summat, an' when Ah think it safe Ah'll gie ye a shove, an' ye can climb in an' pull the hap ower ye."

Coralina did as she was bid, and within moments, the cart was trundling away and Mary ran back to where their cart was parked. Coralina's heart was thumping in her chest; she was terrified that at any moment she would hear her father's voice yelling for them to stop. Tears coursed down her face and she sobbed, her heart breaking at the thought of never seeing her sister again. Robert had led the horses down the hill from Neilston into Barrhead and was heading down through Crookston before he felt it was safe enough to stop for a moment to make sure that Coralina was all right, hidden under the hap as she was. He swung round on the bench and lifted a corner of the cover, "Are ye a'right Coralina?" He was shocked when her face appeared, her eyes red, tear streaked and swollen from crying. "Oh ma darlin' Ah canny bide here, but in a wee while it will be safe for us tae stop for a minute. Take a drink o' water from the flask, it'll be a'right." Now he was overwhelmed with guilt and fear wondering if he had done the right thing, beginning to question his choice and fearing for Coralina wondering if she would ever get over her grief. He had decided that they would camp out for the night near Erskine, and then the next day they would take the ferry across the Clyde and travel on towards Loch Lomond. He knew they would need to travel far to be safe from Coralina's Gypsy family and if necessary they would go as far as Fort William and beyond. He would do whatever it took to make a happy and safe life for himself and Coralina.

From Crookston he followed the road to Renfrew and beyond until he found a suitable place to stop. He was keen to share this with Coralina. He settled his two horses, tethering them loosely to allow them to graze and went back to the cart. Coralina was sound asleep under the hap; he lifted a corner and as he gazed at her, he was overwhelmed with his love for her.

"Coralina, wake up sweetheart," he touched her shoulder gently "It's jist me, we're safe' dinnae be scared, sit up, come an' see."

Coralina rubbed her eyes, sat up and looked out over the edge of the cart. "Oh my, that's jist lovely, where are wi'?"

"Erskine, and that's Dumbarton Castle yonder. Come on, ye should stretch yer legs, let's take a walk an' then Ah'll make a fire an' wi' can have some tea an' a bit tae eat."

They walked hand in hand with the sun shining on them, admiring the view and as Robert placed his arm around Coralina's shoulders, she felt a sense of security. He kissed her there for the first time, standing on the hill above the Clyde and she knew that she loved him with all her heart and she knew that he would always take care of her.

Chapter 21

It was almost noon before John realised that something was amiss. He kept questioning Mary, and although she was resilient, before long she was in tears. He was frantic with worry, "Ye know summat, Ah'm sure ye know summat Mary, an' if ye dinnae tell me Ah'll whip yer hide."

"Ah dinnae ken Da, Ah was watchin' the fair, Ah didnae see whur she went."

"If yer hidin' summat fae me, Ah'll never forgive ye Mary, ye'll pay for this Mary, one way or t'other ye'll pay for this."

All Mary could do was stand and cry. She cried for her sister knowing that she would probably never see her again, and she cried for her father, for his anger and contempt of her. John went around the fairground several times. He asked people he knew, and he asked strangers if they had seen his lass. Other Gypsies began to congregate around him offering to set up a search party. Some made their way down to Barrhead and Darnley others went on to Uplawmoor, but no one had seen anything.

Two weeks had passed since that day at the Neilston Fair. Each day her father rode off searching for Coralina. Each night he came back more dejected than before. All thoughts of attending fairs or going for supplies were pushed to one side. After another long day searching John rode into camp, young Johnny took his horse and led it away to attend to it, and John went over to sit by the fire that was set in the middle of the camp. He took a bottle from his jacket pocket and drank from it. The whisky burned as it went down but he felt nothing but the pain in his heart.

The atmosphere in the camp was subdued, and day by day the number of folk who had been searching had whittled away. Those who lived on the camp were reluctant to ask John if there was any news, there was no need really as they could see by his face that he had discovered nothing.

Mary was isolated in her despair, it was as though the life had gone out of her and it felt as though everyone blamed her. John knew that some of Coralina's belongings were gone, so he knew too that she hadn't been taken. Wherever she was she had planned to go, John was certain that Mary must know something about it, but Mary had given her word, and she refused to admit that she knew anything, not even to young Johnny.

Isabella was making a pot of tea one morning and seeing John coming out of his wagon, ready to begin another days searching, she called to him.

"Have some tea afore ye go John."

John walked over and sat beside her at the fire. Trying to get John back to normal life, she asked if he would be going for supplies soon and the effect was startling. John stared at her for a moment, but that moment seemed like an eternity.

"That's it!" he said, as he jumped up, spilling his tea as the cup was thrown to the ground, "That's whur she is!"

Isabella was startled and she jumped up too, "Whur dae ye think she is John?"

"Away wi' Robert Miller!" he said, as he ran off to fetch his horse.

Isabella was left standing open mouthed as she watched John race off. He was saddled up within a few minutes and riding out of the camp at speed. All she could do now was wait and wonder. Mary, seeing the exchange and her father riding off at speed ran towards Isabella, “Whit’s up wi’ ma Da?”

“Yer Da thinks Coralina’s wi’ the Miller’s!”

Mary stood there, fear written over her face.

“Dae ye ken summat Mary? If ye dae ye better tell me.”

“Ah dinnae ken onythin’.”

“Well if ye ken summat’ ye better tell me afore yer Da comes back.”

Mary turned and walked away, leaving Isabella standing by the fire wondering if Coralina was away with Robert Miller, and if she was she thought it was her fault because she encouraged John to take her with him to Dalgarven. She thought that John would be furious with her.

The trauma that Mary had endured over the past few weeks was plain to see. Her puppy fat had disappeared largely due to the fact that she had lost her appetite and wasn’t sleeping. She kept worrying about how her sister was, and she feared that her father would never speak to her again. It wasn’t her fault, but she felt as though everyone was shunning her as though it was. She didn’t understand why she was being blamed; she was still there, it was Coralina who had run away, but that’s the way it is with people when they are hurt, angry or afraid, they take their angst out on those who are closest to them regardless of whether they are responsible or not.

Confused and upset, she left the camp and made her way to the horse field and called Mizzie, who was at the other end of the field grazing. Mizzie was sulking, and not prepared to jump to Mary’s call, after all she had been neglecting her recently. She called again and Mizzie, lifted her head, gave her a look, and then carried on grazing.

It was just too much to bear. Mary dropped to her knees on the grass, and with her head in her hands she cried her heart out. A few moments later she felt a warm moist tickle on the back of her neck, and startled, she looked up as Mizzie nuzzled her once more. That only made her cry some more, she thought her heart would break. Mizzie nudged her, and Mary stood up and rested her face against Mizzie's neck. The horse snorted and huffed at her, and Mary hauled herself onto her back and rode to the edge of the roped off area. She dismounted, and untying the rope she led Mizzie out of the field, jumped on once more, and rode off across the fields. Johnny had been watching from a distance, and as soon as he realised that she was taking Mizzie out he ran to the field and followed her on one of the other horses.

She cried as she rode, and her mind was preoccupied with thoughts of Coralina and of her Da. She had no thought or idea of where she was going, and she wouldn't have cared anyway. She felt lost, lonely, and alone, and things would never be as they were before. She followed the river, passing the log that she had sat on with her sister on many occasions, but she didn't stop there. She continued to follow the river for another two miles from the camp. Finally, exhaustion set in and Mary slowed Mizzie down to a walk, and led her to a small clearing beside a large oak tree. She dismounted and walked Mizzie to the water's edge to drink.

Johnny followed at a distance; he knew she was hurting but he didn't know how to fix that, all he could do was follow in case she needed him, or in case she hurt herself. When he saw her by the river, he dismounted and walked over to stand beside her. She saw Johnny approaching but she didn't speak, nor did he. When Mizzie had taken what she needed Johnny took her by her head collar, and led her and his own horse to a nearby tree, tying them so that they could graze but wouldn't wander off. He turned to see Mary, sitting there on the grass under the oak tree, knees bent, her arms resting on her knees and her head resting on her arms. Her long dark hair hid her face, but he knew that she was crying. He went over and sat beside her, and there they sat quietly together, neither saying anything to the other. Finally, Johnny spoke, "Dae ye want tae tell me onythin'."

Mary shook her head.

"Talk tae me Mary, dae ye ken whur yer sister is?"

Mary didn't answer, but Johnny asked again, "Dae ye ken whur yer sister is Mary?"

She looked him straight in the eye and truthfully told him that she didn't, she wasn't lying, she didn't know where Coralina was. Johnny shook his head sadly. "Mary Ah've known ye all ma life an' Ah've seen the best o' ye an' the worst o' ye. There is nothin' that ye can say tae me that will shock me, an' if yer worried that Ah'll tell yer Da then you dinnae gie me credit. Talk tae me Mary, tell me whit's in yer mind."

Mary started to sob once more, "Ma sisters away an' ma' Da's no' speaking tae me, an' Ah canny bear it."

Johnny wrapped his arm around her shoulder and pulled her towards him, and slowly they sank backwards to lie on the grass together. Johnny held her in an embrace and whispered into her hair, "Ah love ye Mary Kelly, ye have nothin' tae fear 'cause Ah'll watch oot for ye."

They lay on the grass for a while until Mary's sobbing had subsided, but although she trusted Johnny with her life, she held on to her secret for a while yet. The time would come when she would share, but not yet.

Chapter 22

Robert had left a short note for Elsie and Mathew to find after he had left. It just said, *'Ma an' Da Ah'm sorry tae tell ye that Ah've had tae go away. Don't worry aboot me. Ah'll be in touch as soon as Ah'm settled. Love Robert.'*

They were worried sick, and couldn't understand why he had left, and his note gave no explanation. They had always done their best by him, and he had always been a good son; they were mystified as to why he would leave. As is usual when people do not know the true facts, their minds go into overdrive and begin to imagine all manner of problems. For two weeks they fretted and argued about the reasons why he might have gone, and then out of the blue, when they least expected, a letter arrived. Elsie was in her kitchen kneading dough for bread when the postman stuck his head round her door, "A letter for ye Elsie."

"Eh? Whit's that? Jist put it on the table," she said, holding up her hands covered in dough to demonstrate why she couldn't take it. As soon as he was gone, she grabbed a cloth and started to wipe the dough from her hands. Thinking that it might be word about Robert, she looked at it as though it would burst into flames, and then ran to fetch Mathew from the mill.

"Mathew! Mathew! Come quick."

On hearing her urgent call, Mathew rushed from the mill, "Whit's up wi' ye wummin'?"

"A letter!" she said, hurrying him back to the kitchen. At first they stood and looked at it, till Mathew picked it up and began to read it to Elsie, who was wringing her hands in distress.

'Dear Ma an' Da, Ah'm sorry aboot the way Ah had tae leave, an' Ah wish things could'ha' been different. Ah aye thought Ah would spend ma life at the mill. Ah thought Ah would bring ma wife tae the mill and start a family there, but ye see that was nae tae be. Ye see there is nae other lass for me but Coralina Kelly, an' wi' widnae get her Da's permission tae wed, so wi' have left tae make oor ane life an' maybe wan day wi'll see ye again. Ah huvnae dishonoured Coralina so ye dinnae need tae be ashamed o' me. Wi'll be merried soon. Ye'll aye be in ma thoughts an' prayers. Ah'll be in touch soon

Yer ever lovin' son Robert.'

Elsie sat down, slumped at the table. Mathew stood by her side, both of them in shock.

"Ah dinnae ken if that's a blessin' or a curse," said Mathew.

"It's no' a curse, how could it be a curse."

"Because John Kelly will go crazy when he finds oot."

"It's been two weeks Mathew, he must surely ken."

"Aye, he'll ken she's away, but he might no' ken that she's away wi' oor Robert, and when he does ken…"

Mathew shook his head in despair.

"Whit dae ye think he'll dae?" asked Elsie.

"Who can say, he might try tae find them, an' if he does they could gang up on oor Robert. It's been hard wi' Robert away, it could be harder still if the Gypsies stop buying fae us."

"Dae ye think wi' should try tae get in touch wi' him?"

"Tae tell him his lassie has ran away wi' oor Robert!" asked Mathew in disbelief.

"Ah widnae like tae think he would dae onythin' bad, but Ah widnae like tae think he is worryin' himsel' sick aboot where she might be."

The words were no sooner out of their mouths than they heard him coming, the horse's hoofs clattering on the yard as he rode in.

"Leave this tae me Elsie," said Mathew, as he went to the door.

John was dismounting, and seeing Mathew, he turned and asked accusingly, "Where are they? Ah'm tellin ye man, Ah dinnae want tae hurt ye, but ye better tell me where ma lass is."

Ever the diplomat Mathew replied, "Come away in John."

John was in no mood for niceties but, had little option if he wanted to find out where his daughter was.

"Make some tea Elsie, sit yer self doon John."

"Ah'll stand," it was apparent by his face that he would not take kindly to platitudes and they could smell the stale whisky on him.

"She's no' here John, this letter jist came. Wi' were jist havin' a look at it as ye arrived." He slid the letter across the table to John. For a moment John looked at the letter, and then he looked across the table to Mathew, "That's nae use tae me, for Ah cannae read."

Mathew took the letter back and John slumped in the chair as Mathew read it to him.

"She has shamed me an' the rest o' the family."

"Ye heard it yirsel John, in ma son's words, he didnae dishonour her."

"That's as may be, but she's dishonoured her family, for she's meant tae merry her ain kind."

"It's no' that bad man, can ye no' jist accept it, after a' we're be gonnae be family, an' there'll be bairns in the future."

The words were hardly uttered from Mathew's mouth when John stood up, knocking over the chair that he had been sitting in. He yelled at Mathew, "Family! Family! Ye'll never be part o' ma family! Nor will ma lass! Never! Never again! As far as Ah'm concerned, she's dead tae me an' mine." He scrunched the letter in his hand and threw it to the floor, before making his way to the door, and at the last second he turned and said, "Ye'll no' see oor kind again either, we'll be getting oor needs elsewhere."

Mathew picked up the letter and smoothed it out, and then walked over to comfort Elsie who was standing by the kitchen sink quietly crying. They listened to the sound of John riding away, both of them afraid of what the future would bring. Reading between the lines, if John considered that Coralina was dead to him, then perhaps he would be less likely to try to find them, but still there was a chance that he might go looking with the rest of his camp and the outcome of that would be dire. They also knew that at their time of life they would be unable to continue to carry the heavy burden of running the mill for much longer without Roberts' support.

"Ah've never known him tae smell of the drink Elsie, have you?"

"Naw, no' in a' the time he has been comin' here. Ah think he might be hittin' the bottle hard."

On John's return to the camp he was met by Isabella. She could see he was enraged, and knew that things had not gone well, she was cautious about speaking to him, but knew that she must say something.

"Are' ye gonnae tell me whit's whit'?"

"Wan thing," he said, turning on her and pointing his finger at her, "Never mention her name tae me again." And with that he turned and walked away, leaving Isabella to wonder what he had found out.

It was Isabella's responsibility now to make sure that everyone knew not to mention Coralina, and of course everyone wanted to know what he had found out, but no one dared to ask John, and Isabella was unable to make them any the wiser. It was only later, drunk on the whisky and rambling like a man possessed, that others found out that Coralina had run away with the miller's son.

Part 2 Mary's Story

Chapter 23

Everything changed after Coralina ran away. John seldom spoke to anyone except young Johnny. He hardly looked at Mary and only spoke to her if he had to; he no longer trusted her, and he blamed her. Initially Mary was badly affected by her father's reaction, but she was made of stronger stuff, nevertheless the experience changed her. Before, Mary was confident, outgoing, determined, and capable of doing whatever she wanted, and although inwardly she still retained these strengths they were tempered with a seriousness, a quietness, that was difficult for anyone around her to penetrate. She seldom conversed with anyone any more, except for Johnny, and she spent most of her time doing only what she had to do. Mary was always found around the horses when her tasks were done, but she and her father avoided each other, and the general atmosphere around them was uncomfortable.

John, like many others on the camp, had always enjoyed a bottle of beer or an occasional nip or two of whisky, but since Coralina's departure, John had taken to 'the hard stuff' and was often the worse for wear. His cousin Willie, Johnny's father and his brother-in-law George did their best to talk to him about his drinking but eventually they considered him a lost cause and they watched as he neglected his responsibilities, and left young Johnny to pick up the slack. In some ways, this was a blessing for Mary because it was easier for her to be involved in helping with the horses when it was just her and Johnny. Soon even the responsibility of selling the horses and fetching the provisions fell on Johnny's shoulders, while John slouched somewhere in a drunken stupor.

Hard work had toughened young Johnny, he had filled out and matured beyond his years. Anyone seeing the seventeen-year-old would have assumed that he was in his early twenties. In looks, he was handsome, lean though muscular and tall. He still had some growing to do, but he was already taller than his peers were. He had dark hair typical in his family but his eyes were a piercing blue and they often conveyed more than his words did. When Johnny wasn't focused on his work load, his attention was always on Mary and he looked for her if she wasn't close by.

Each day Mary seemed to grow more striking. At fifteen she had lost her childlike looks and was blossoming into a beautiful young woman. She carried herself with grace and dignity as though she was better than everyone else, but really her appearance and attitude belied her inner grief, and all she was doing was protecting herself from the opinions that others may have had of her. She was every bit a typical Gypsy lass with cascading dark hair and the darkest eyes. Mary preferred her own company when she wasn't around Johnny and of late, she had taken to solitary night time walks in the moonlight. Spending time alone sharpened her gift of the sight and with each passing day she was becoming more gifted, though she had learned from experience to keep her impressions to herself.

The Moon fascinated her and she was sure that it wasn't a man in the moon that she could see; she was certain it was a woman; she called her 'The Lady'. Sometimes in the night under the full of the moon she would stand there with her arms spread wide and implore The Lady of the Moon to guide her, to help her to understand her life. She would ask for help to stop her father drinking so much and she would ask that her sister would always be safe and happy. No one told her what to do when she was on her moonlight walks and no one had told her how to chant in rhyme but natural instincts took over and became habit. Perhaps it was hidden in the words of the old Mither and how she made them repeat rhymes about plants and their uses.

Mary now had rhymes for every occasion and was quick to create new rhymes whenever she required them.

For wisdom and understanding she would chant,

'Borage with your heed cast doon

Take away ma worried froon

An' sage ye guide, tell me whit's right

Tae still ma worries on this night.'

Sometimes she would seek out dried petals from flowers and plants that she had gathered and occasionally if she didn't have what she needed she would ask Mither Isabella if she had any to spare. Off she would go and sit by the river and grind her petals or seed mixture until it was little more than a fine dust and then she would chant her rhyme and set a light to the dust.

Her thoughts often drifted back to that day that she had spent with the old Mither when she first found out that the old Mither knew that she knew things and could see things. She worried about what bad things would come back to her because she had helped Coralina to run away. She did not think that helping Coralina was a bad thing, but her father blamed her, and she thought everyone else did too. She was more mindful of her reactions to anything that displeased her, afraid of what the consequences might be, but now and again her temper would rise. Others in the camp would approach her if they were feeling poorly as they knew she had a healing gift, but wherever there is a positive, there is always a negative to bring balance.

On one occasion Daisy, Isabella's youngest daughter, taunted Mary as she was walking by.

"Ah dinnae ken why that Johnny bothers wi' ye Mary Kelly wi' yer nose stuck in the air, he'd be better aff wi' wan o' us," she called out after her.

Mary turned, glared at her and pointed her finger in Daisy's direction and then just as suddenly, she dropped her hand, turned and hurried away.

Later Daisy related the event to her sisters and anyone else who would listen. "Ah'm tellin' ye, she pointed at ma stomach an' Ah got such a pain an' Ah had the skitters a' day. It was her, Ah'm tellin' ye. Ah was trippen' ower ma self goin' back an' furrat tae the dunny!"

Eventually the gossip got back to Johnny.

"Ah thought ye were by that stuff Mary? Dae ye ken whit Daisy's sayin'?"

"Aye Ah've heard, an' she's talkin' rubbish, Ah didnae dae anythin, Ah nearly did but Ah stopped ma self. It's no' that when they have summat wrang or they want a potion, they come tae me for healin', or when they're hopin tae charm a fella."

When the other girls and women were going around the doors selling doilies and sprigs of flowers to make some money, Mary was telling fortunes, and word travels fast when you are good at something like that. Often when the others would have a door slammed in their face, Mary would have housewives eagerly waiting to hear what she had to tell them. The other girls were jealous of Mary. Apart from her demeanour, she always made more money than they did. Having more money meant that she could buy cloth for dresses or skirts and since Coralina had gone away Mary had started to make her own clothes, with difficulty at first but then with experience she became quite adept at her new skill.

Chapter 24

Mary missed Coralina desperately, and had eventually confided in Johnny that she had known about her father's plans to marry Coralina off and how upset Coralina was at the thought. She had asked Johnny how he would have felt if she had to marry someone else. Johnny stood there looking down at her for she was shorter than he was, and said with finality, "It would never happen."

After Mary's explanation of her reasons for helping her sister, Johnny began to call in at Dalgarven, to speak to the Millers, enquiring if there was any word from Coralina and Robert, although he knew that it was forbidden. Initially, the Millers were understandably cautious, but over time they began to realise that Johnny meant no ill will, instead he was anxious to carry word of Coralina's wellbeing back to Mary. He never ever mentioned to John or anyone other than Mary anything that the Millers told him. Soon it became apparent that this was a good way for Mary and Coralina to keep in touch, albeit sporadically. Mathew was able to tell Johnny that Robert and Coralina had a little girl named Emily. Johnny was certain that the Millers knew where Robert and Coralina were, and was just as certain that they had visited them wherever they were, but the Millers gave nothing more away.

On one of his visits Mathew told Johnny that Coralina had been asking if he and Mary were wed yet. This had been on Johnny's mind for some time, but John was in a such a permanent state of drunkenness, that Johnny had been putting off the idea of setting a date. It was a foregone conclusion that he and Mary would wed, it was just a matter of time, but Mary held out hope that her father would sober up. That wasn't to be, his health just worsened with the effects of alcohol poisoning. Mary cared for her father; she washed his soiled clothes, she fed him soup when he was too drunk to care about eating, and she covered him to keep him warm when he fell over too drunk to even know where he was.

She found him late one February night lying out in the open. It was so cold that the grass was stiff and his clothes were almost frozen onto him. She ran for Johnny who helped her to get him up and back to the wagon. Together they stripped him out of his sodden clothes and put him to bed after bathing him down with cloths soaked in warm water, but the damage was already done. Eventually he was so ill that he couldn't get out of his bed, but even that wasn't too much for Mary. She cleaned his mess and washed him, tried to coax him to eat, and prepared syrups to ease his rasping cough. Every time she attended to him her heart broke a little bit more, remembering the man he had been, until finally he was breathing his last.

Johnny was in the wagon with Mary, and he watched as the love of his life grieved for the father she had lost years before. He grieved with her, remembering all the good times that they had shared and travelled together. Everything he knew, he knew because this man had taught him. Mary sat cradling her father in her arms holding him up to try to ease his breathing when suddenly his breathing became quick and shallow and he gasped for air.

"Da! Da!" Mary screamed, "Oh Da! Dinnae leave me, take ma breath, Da take ma breath." And her father opened his eyes; he looked tenderly into Mary's eyes, clutched her hand, and drew it to his lips. He kissed her hand and closed his eyes never to open them again. Mary crumpled over her father sobbing uncontrollably and all Johnny could do was sit and watch as he too wept for what was lost. Eventually her tears spent she stood and made to leave the wagon.

"Where are ye goin' Mary?" he asked catching her arm. She turned and looked him in the eyes then looked down at his hand on her arm holding her back.

"Let me be Johnny," she said and as he released his grip, she turned and left the wagon. She ran across the field and through the trees until she reached the river. She found her way by instinct rather than sight because it was a black night in the dark of the moon. She knelt by the river filled with a rage that was so powerful that she felt her heart would burst. Without intention, her mouth opened and she released a guttural scream as she looked up at the dark sky looking for the Moon. Then she yelled,

"Aye hide yer face pretend ye cannae see

But take this, it's the last ye'll hear fae me

Ye took ma sister an' then ye took ma Da

The next time Ah see ye Ah'll hide ma face an' a'."

She cried until she was empty.

Johnny's father Willie came into the wagon to comfort his son for he knew that he had been a great influence in Johnny's life and of course, he grieved too, for he was losing a dearly loved cousin. Willie stayed in the wagon until Johnny went looking for Mary. He knew where she would be and was not surprised to find her on the ground, shivering with the cold, staring blindly ahead of her. No words passed between them as he gently coaxed her to her feet and took her to Isabella's.

Father and son were stoic in their grief over the next few days, as they prepared John for his final resting place at Janefield Cemetery.

"Will ye keep her wi' ye Isabella for wi' have tae burn that wagon?"

"Dinnae worry yer self aboot that Johnny, Ah'll see tae her."

"Ah have a wagon comin' for us when wi' get merried but Ah don't think wi' should dae it till some time has passed and she has been able tae deal wi' her grief."

"Aye lets jist get this ower wi' first."

The following days were a blur to Mary, she couldn't think, she couldn't eat and she couldn't sleep. She wandered, like a zombie, back and forward between the horses and the river that she loved to sit by, her eyes staring straight ahead avoiding any eye contact with anyone. When the first sliver of the Moon appeared, she felt a deep guilt and wandered back to the river.

"Silver Lady in the sky

Ah've come tae tell ye ma tears are dry

Ah'm sorry Ah was awfy bad

Ah didnae mean it, grief made me mad.

Ah'll Aye come back tae talk tae ye

Please Lady dinnae look away."

Just as she was saying those last words, a cloud passed over the moon and hid it from her sight and her heart filled with sadness and dread.

After John's funeral Mary moved into Isabella and George's wagon, much to the displeasure of Daisy. Nellie had only recently married Willie's nephew,

Edward McGuigan, who was a skilled carpenter, and Jennie had gone with her husband to live at another camp after their wedding, so it was just Daisy still in the wagon with her parents. In spite of them both sharing the same breast milk when they were babies, the two girls did not have a good word for each other. Daisy felt sorry for Mary's loss, but that didn't mean that she had to like sharing her home with her. She had nothing to worry about because Mary was too grief stricken to care or think about Daisy or anyone else for that matter.

Their wagon was gone now, it had been taken away and burned with everything in it, and she hadn't even a keepsake to hold, to remind her of happier times. Johnny had hardly any time for her because he was tending to her father's responsibilities, seeing to the horses and now that the worst of the winter had passed, travelling here and there fetching provisions for the camp. He had found the time to call into Dalgarven to ask the Millers if they would pass word to Coralina about her father's passing.

"Ah'm right sorry tae hear that," said Mathew.

"Aye, it's been hard on Mary an' she's no' taken it well. Ah expect that Coralina will be saddened tae."

"He jist never got over Coralina runnin' away."

"Naw, it fair broke his heart."

Johnny was leaving when the Millers surprised him with another piece of news.

"Afore ye go Johnny, Ah jist wanted tae tell ye if ye come tae see us again, come tae that last cottage on the Beith Road for me an' Elsie are givin' up the mill an' another family will be runnin it. It's too hard with oot Robert and we're retiring fae it."

Robert leaving with Coralina had wide reaching effects, and Johnny couldn't help but wonder how things would have turned out if there had been another way. A big part of him thought that what they had done was selfish considering the consequences, but at the same time he wondered how he and Mary would have acted under the same circumstances. He knew that he would give up everything for his Mary and he couldn't imagine his life without her in it.

Chapter 25

As the days passed, Mary found comfort in going over to Nellie's wagon keeping her company and enjoying baby Eddie. More often than not, she just sat quietly cradling Eddie in her arms, but she didn't shy away from carrying soiled nappies to the dunny or rinsing them off in the river before they would be boiled. Nellie had the same temperament as her mother and never ever pushed Mary to talk unless Mary started a conversation. The silence and the time spent with little Eddie were healing for Mary. Gradually, day by day, her appetite picked up and she began to feel like her old self. She began once more to enjoy Johnny's company and spending time around the horses, particularly Mizzie.

No one was more surprised than Johnny when a few weeks later, Mary suddenly announced to him, "It's time we were wed Johnny and Ah dinnae want any fuss, jist here, in the camp, but Ah want tae be wed on the first o' May. Dae whit ye have tae dae tae make it happen," and with that parting comment she turned and walked away. Johnny stood looking after her, shaking his head but with a wide grin on his face, then he ran after her and grabbing her by the arm, he spun her around and kissed her passionately on the lips. He took Mary's breath away and some of the children nearby started hooping and cheering and laughing. Mary, being Mary just gave him a look and walked off again but her heart was pounding in her chest and for the first time in months, she felt whole and happy in herself.

"Ah'm gettin' wed!" she thought excitedly to herself *"Ah wish ma sister was here."* For a moment, she felt her emotions overwhelming her and she wanted so desperately to cry but she had cried enough over the last few years and she didn't give in to her feelings. Later that night under a full moon, Mary went out as usual and sitting by the river, she made her wish.

"Bairns Ah want for Johnny an' me

Not one but two maybe even three

Tae be a guid mither is ma intent

An' wi' this dust ma wish is sent

A lassie or two tae bide by me

A laddie for Johnny would make the three

Ah'll teach the lassies whit they need tae know

The laddie wi' Johnny will aye go

Ah ask this on a moonlit night

Under the stars that shine sae bright

A guid wife an' mither is ma intent

An wi' this dust ma wish is sent"

At times like these, Mary felt whole and content and when she returned to the wagon, she did so with a soft smile on her lips. The next day she made her way to Nellie's wagon and went in to give her the news.

"Ah'm right happy for ye Mary, ye'll have tae start thinkin aboot whit tae wear. First o' May, there'll be flowers oot that ye can put in yer hair an' ye'll look bonny."

"Ah have a nice bit o' cloth tae make a dress for ma weddin'."

A bale of red cotton at one of the fairs had captivated Mary and she had bought herself enough to make a dress. She hadn't yet done anything with it, but she decided there and then that this was what she would use to make her new dress.

Nellie was looking at her as though she had something to say, "Whit's up Nellie?"

"Nothin', Ah wis jist thinkin' that would be nice."

Mary was puzzled by the look, but too excited with her own thoughts to pay much heed. After Mary left, Nellie went across to see her mother.

"Mam Ah think we have a wee problem."

"Whit's up Nellie?"

"Did ye no' tell me that after Auntie Mary Ellen died, Uncle John gave ye her weddin dress for safe keepin'?"

"Aye Ah did, that was a long time ago, Ah'm surprised ye remember that. Ah'm gonnae get it looked oot an' freshen it up for Mary. She'll be ever so pleased when Ah show it tae her."

"Mary's got some red cloth an' is talkin' about makin' her dress herself."

Isabella stood looking at her; that was a problem, she didn't want to take away Mary's hope of making her own dress, but she didn't want to hide that she had her mother's wedding dress for safekeeping.

"Oh whit tae dae, whit tae dae," said Isabella.

They both sat quietly pondering the problem, trying to think of a suitable solution and then Isabella said, "Don't say a word tae her, jist let her make her dress an when the time is right Ah'll offer her Ma's dress.

In the following days and weeks, when the weather permitted, if Mary wasn't helping Johnny or Nellie with little Eddie, she would gather her fabric, needles threads and scissors and take herself of to sit by the river and put together the dress for her wedding.

No one threw anything away in those days, buttons or fasteners were unpicked from clothes that were beyond repair, patches were cut out and saved, for they were always handy, and trimmings were saved like treasures. Everyone would have a tin full of buttons and fasteners, and a bag full of bits of trimmings and beads. Some were happy to share while others would guard their treasures, unwilling to share them in case they would need them for their own repairs or projects later.

Mary had Coralina's sewing things, and in amongst her treasures she found a bag of beads. She opened the bag and to her delight discovered a broken hematite necklace that she supposed Coralina had found discarded somewhere. As she sat there by the river, she examined the dark grey stones with a silvery sheen and was thrilled to see the way they caught the light. She decided that she would use these beads on the neckline of her dress. Each day when she was finished her task she would fold up her precious workings and wrap them in brown paper then carry them back to the wagon. She was tired of sharing a space, though she was grateful to her aunt and uncle for welcoming her and looking after her. *'One day soon, Ah'll have ma ain wagon an' it'll jist be me an' Johnny,'* she thought to herself as she hid her bundle under the thin mattress on the bed she shared with Daisy, before going over to spend a while with Nellie.

"How are ye getting' on wi' makin' yer dress Mary?"

"Ah'm happy wi' it Nellie Ah think Johnny will like it tae."

"Will ye tell me whit it's like Mary?"

"Ah cannae dae that Nellie, Ah dinnae want onybody to know whit it's like or tae see it afore ma weddin' day."

Nellie laughed, she didn't think that Mary would tell her anything anyway.

Chapter 26

Mary was heading back to the wagon and there was Daisy, sitting on the wooden steps and blocking her way. She had a smug look on her face and Mary felt like slapping her, but she resisted the temptation and said, "Mind yer self, let me by Daisy."

"Whit, are ye too fat tae squeeze by? Naw it cannae be that yer like a stick. That Johnny'll no' have onythin' tae haud on tae come May.

Mary felt her rage rising as she tried to squeeze by Daisy without touching her but Daisy was determined to annoy her.

"Ah suppose ye think that ye'll look good on yer weddin' day in a red dress?"

Mary stopped dead in her tracks half in and half out of the wagon. A raging mist descended on her as she stood there, and that moment seemed like an eternity as she stared at the bed where she had stored her parcel. She rushed to lift the mattress, the brown paper parcel was still there, but she knew that Daisy had tampered with. She let out such a scream of rage that Daisy, who had been so bold previously, leapt from the step, and as she landed on the grass, she turned to face Mary who was now in the doorway of the wagon. Before Daisy could think or speak, Mary launched herself on her screaming like a banshee.

"Ya' jealous bitch Ah'll scratch yer eyes oot," she screamed as she landed on her cousin knocking her to the ground. Daisy tried to scramble away on her hands and knees, but Mary was on her again ripping at her hair and trying to draw her nails on any part of Daisy's skin that she could reach.

Hearing the commotion, everyone hurried over to watch the spectacle. Daisy managed to get to her feet and began to run, but nothing was going to hold Mary back not even those who tried to make a grab for her, and she took off after Daisy, who ran like a hare in fear of what Mary might do next. Through the trees she ran, with Mary in hot pursuit. Mary caught up with her as she reached the river, she grabbed her by the hair, spun her around, and threw her with all her might. Daisy spun, tripping over her own feet and tumbled head first in to the river. Mary, not quite finished, ran in after her. Who knows what would have happened next if some of the men hadn't arrived, and what at first seemed amusing, now looked as though it was really getting out of hand as the two girls wrestled with each other, both of them soaked to the skin.

George dragged his daughter away and over to where Isabella stood open mouthed in amazement, "Ye deserve everything ye got Daisy 'cause ye have needled that lassie forever, noo get back tae the wagon an' Ah'll see tae ye later."

Johnny had taken hold of Mary; she looked like a wild woman, her eyes wide with anger, and her hair all over the place. He took her further upstream as everyone else dispersed to sit round the fire and chatter about what they had just witnessed.

"It had tae happen," said one.

"That Daisy's been askin for that for a while an' she should ha' known better than tae take Mary on."

Johnny sat by the river with Mary "Dae ye want tae tell me whit happened?"

Mary was crying her face red from the exertion and the rage that was only now beginning to subside. "She was in at ma weddin' dress Johnny, an' threw it in ma face making feel… Ah don't know whit she made me feel. Ah'm sorry Johnny, Ah'm sorry that yer angry wi' me."

"Ah'm no' angry wi' ye Mary, Ah'm jist worried aboot ye. Wash yer face Mary an' take a drink o' water."

It was days before the atmosphere of the episode with Mary and Daisy settled. Mary set a bender up near the wagon and planned to sleep there until her wedding. She kept herself busy preparing her dress, helping Johnny, or chatting with Nellie. Daisy avoided her if she could and tried to keep a low profile, averting her eyes any time Mary was nearby. Night times, sitting around the campfire, were probably the worst because neither wanted to see or look at the other, but living in such close proximity made that difficult. Eventually something had to give and Mary made the first move. There was bated breath as she walked over to where Daisy was sitting. Daisy saw her coming and her stomach clenched as she wondered what was going to happen. Mary stood and looked down at her cousin "Can Ah sit by ye Daisy?" Daisy's eyes were wide with disbelief. She shuffled along the bench she was sitting on and made room for Mary who without another word on the matter sat down. For a moment, conversation in the group hushed, and everyone was looking around at each other. Eventually Mary said to Daisy "Ah'm goin' for tea will Ah bring you some?"

"Aye!" said Daisy in surprise," and watched, confused, while Mary went to the big teakettle and began to pour two cups of tea.

"Ah hope she disnae pour it on her heid," laughed one.

"Ah hope they put this nonsense behind them," said another.

When Mary took the tea back and handed the cup to Daisy, she sat down beside her. They were silent for a while as the murmuring and chatter resumed around them, but although everyone pretended that they weren't watching, all eyes were on them. Then Daisy said, "Ah'm right sorry for goin' in tae yer parcel an' lookin' at yer dress Mary, an' Ah'm sorry for makin' a fool o' it." Mary turned and looked her in the eye,

"Why did ye?"

"Ah don't know, Ah think Ah was jist jealous," said Daisy, and hung her head sadly.

"Jealous? Ye were jealous o' me. Whit is there tae be jealous o'."

Mary knew that feeling; she could remember the trouble that it caused. She slipped her hand over Daisy's and in hushed tones, she told her about the day that she spent years ago with the old Mither. Daisy was as bewildered as Mary had been so she explained to Daisy. "It's like the music, when the string on the fiddle breaks the music is still there but it sounds bad. When you get angry or jealous the music that's in the air gets sour an' bad things happen."

Daisy absorbed this new information and as she was mulling it over Mary said "Ah've nae Mam, ma sister ran away wi' her fella, Ah've buried ma Da, how can ye be jealous. We should be like sisters you and me; your Mam fed me her milk, sometimes you on wan titty, an' me on the other Ah've heard them say." Mary was smiling as she said this and looking at Daisy she was happy when she saw a giggle escape from her. The two girls sat there holding hands, closer than they had ever been.

"Will ye stand wi' me as ma maid Daisy?" Daisy looked into Mary's eyes and both girls had tears forming. "Aye Mary, Ah will, thanks for askin' me." At that, both girls threw their arms around each other and everyone present raised their eyebrows in surprise and breathed a sigh of relief. Johnny was so proud of his bride to be and his heart swelled with love for her as he watched the exchange. From that day, the girls never fought again and were as close as sisters should be. They both learned valuable lessons but Mary would pay later for things that had happened, and those things that were yet to materialise.

Chapter 27

All too soon, the wedding day arrived. Isabella, Daisy, and her sister Nellie were fussing over preparations. A circle of stones decorated with wild flowers was set at Mary's favourite spot by the river. Daisy had gathered Bog Myrtle, with its aromatic and aphrodisiac scent for fertility, and Meadowsweet with its profusion of tiny white flowers for love and happiness. These she tied together to make a pretty bouquet, saving some that she fashioned into a garland for Mary's hair. Other women on the camp busied themselves preparing soups and stews for the party and the men busied themselves laying out boards so that the revellers could dance the night away.

Johnny had gone to fetch the new wagon that he would present to Mary during the festivities. In those days, it was legal for a blacksmith to marry couples, so George Morrison would perform the ceremony, he was sitting quietly in Nellie and Edward's wagon going over in his mind the things that he would say to help the happy couple exchange their promises to each other. Isabella, her tasks done went back to her wagon to help Mary get ready. She had just stepped out of the galvi bath and was drying herself off.

"Leave that be, Ah'll empty the bath Mary, jist you get dried for Ah have somethin' tae show ye."

She was standing in the wagon with a loose wrap over her underwear when Isabella came back in, she was carrying a paper parcel. "Sit doon lass. Ah know that ye have been busy makin' yer dress this past wee while an' it's taken yer mind aff things that might have upset ye."

Mary had no idea what was coming and she was beginning to get a little bit worried.

"Whit's up has summat happened tae ma dress?"

"Naw Mary, nothin' like that. Ah jist want tae tell ye summat, but jist remember ye don't need tae feel guilty no matter whit yer choice is."

"Tell me quick Auntie for Ah'm feart noo."

"A long time ago when your Ma died, yer Da came tae me wi' summat tae keep for his lassies. Ah've had it a' this time, an' Ah know Ah could have told ye before ye made yer dress, but it wis makin ye happy an' takin yer mind aff other things so Ah have kept it till noo."

She handed the parcel to Mary but Mary was almost afraid to open it. "Whit is it?"

"It's the dress yer Mam wore on her weddin day."

Mary burst into tears as she opened the paper parcel. She opened the precious contents and could hardly see for the tears streaming down her face. This was the first and only thing that she had ever touched that had been her mothers and her emotions were just brimming over.

She stroked the fine pale blue cotton lawn fabric with tiny sprigs of white daisies all over it. A blue ribbon threaded through the scooped neckline creating a gathered effect and handmade lace edged around the cuffs of the sleeves.

She was crying so much she could hardly speak but through her tears she said, "It's the loveliest thing Ah have ever seen," and looking at her aunt she asked, "Can Ah wear it the day?"

Isabella was crying now and she could remember the day that Mary Ellen had worn it. "Aye, of course ye can wear it, yer no' angry then. Whit aboot yer red dress?"

"Ma red dress, Ah can wear that onytime; Ah can only wear this once an' Ah want tae wear it the day. Thanks Auntie Isabella. Ah dinnae know how tae thank ye for a' ye've done for me these past months."

"Nae need tae thank me Mary, yer jist like wan o' ma ain." Mary stepped forward and gave Isabella a warm hug, "Ah needed tae say thanks, it's meant a lot tae me, an' this is jist so special."

Isabella helped Mary into her mother's dress just as Daisy arrived, garland and bouquet in hand, "Ah made these for ye Mary."

"Oh Daisy that's lovely Ah'm ever so grateful."

"Aw' Mary, ye look fair bonnie in yer Mam's dress. Whit will ye dae wi' yer red dress?"

"Ah'll put it on later for the dancin'," she replied laughing.

Mary's red dress, covered with a cloth to keep dust off it, was hanging on a hook.

"Ye jist look lovely Mary," said Daisy.

Mary was glowing with joy but her stomach was churning with nerves. Isabella reached over and kissed her, as did Nellie, all of them ready to make their way to where the wedding was to take place. It was an emotional time and everyone had tears in their eyes as Mary finished getting ready. "Jist wait a few minutes Mary and then come wi' Daisy."

"Where am Ah goin'?"

"Daisy knows, she'll bring ye," said Isabella as she and Nellie left the wagon. Mary and Daisy stood and looked at each other.

"Ah feel as though Ah've waited for this moment a' ma life Daisy."

"Well it's here noo," said Daisy, "are ye ready to go?"

"Aye, Ah'm ready."

They made their way through the camp towards the trees. "Where are wi' goin' Daisy?"

"Ye'll see in a minute."

"Ah thought wi' would be set up in the middle o' the camp?"

Daisy just looked at her grinning, took her by the hand, and hurried her along. Just as they came to the end of the trees at the edge of the river, Mary caught sight of all her friends and family. Everyone from the camp had gathered and formed two lines for Mary and Daisy to walk through. Mary was blushing and smiling and that was the first sight that Johnny caught of his bride as she walked through the aisle of well-wishers.

Mary realised that she was getting married at her favourite spot by the river and she saw the circle of stones decorated with flowers. Mary and Johnny caught sight of each other at the same time. Johnny thought his heart would burst with pride as he looked at his beautiful bride. Mary's eyes sparkled with love when she saw Johnny in his dark suit, waistcoat, white shirt, and red patterned scarf at his neck. A gold hoop dangled from his ear and his dark curly hair came down over his collar.

Daisy took her straight to Johnny, and he held out his hand for her and together they turned to face their Uncle George who was standing in the middle of the circle. They walked forward together and stood in front of George.

"It's ma duty the day tae witness the joinin' of Johnny Stewart, horse breeder, and Mary Kelly, maiden. Johnny Stewart, dae ye take this lassie, Mary Kelly, as yer wedded wife?"

"Aye, Ah dae, that Ah dae."

"An' you Mary Kelly, dae you take Johnny Stewart, as yer wedded husband?"

"Aye, Ah dae."

"Dae ye have a ring Johnny?" Johnny took a gold band from his pocket.

"Well, put it on her finger and repeat after me, *I Johnny Stewart, do take thee Mary Kelly tae be ma wedded wife, to have and to hold, to honour and care for, tae love and cherish, through sickness an' health till death dae us part.*"

Johnny gazed into Mary's eyes and repeated his vows solemnly.

"An' you Mary repeat after me, *I Mary Kelly do take thee Johnny Stewart, tae be ma wedded husband, to have and to hold, to honour an' obey…*" As George said the words 'honour and obey', there were a few laughs from the gathered crowd, as everyone knew that Mary would find obeying difficult to do. Johnny and Mary laughed too and then Mary without prompting from George, continued her vows with, "Aye, Ah'll obey ye, an' care for ye, Ah'll love and cherish ye through sickness and health till ma last breath."

"Have you got the cord Daisy?" Daisy stepped forward and handed her father a length of white cord, which he proceeded to wrap around Johnny and Mary's joined hands. "With this cord ye are bound together in wedlock, let no man put asunder whit has been joined here the day." There was a long pause as everyone waited; Mary and Johnny were oblivious to everyone but each other.

"Ah now pronounce ye husband an' wife."

There was silence as Mary and Johnny stood gazing into each other's eyes.

"Well man, are ye gonnae kiss her or are ye jist gonnae stand there looking glaikit?" said George and at that Johnny leant down, embraced Mary and kissed her passionately on the lips to the raucous cheering of the gathered crowd.

Then the shouting began, Nellie had placed a broom decorated with flowers and ribbons at the edge of the circle of stones, and everyone was shouting, "Jump the broom, jump the broom, jump the broom." And hands still tied together that's exactly what they did, they jumped the broomstick and took off running through the trees, running and laughing whilst everyone else, laughing hilariously took turns at jumping over the broomstick.

Chapter 28

They could hear everyone laughing and shouting as they ran through the trees. Finally, they found a secluded spot and Johnny held Mary close to him and gazed into her eyes. She could feel his heart pounding in time with hers as he lifted her chin and kissed her on her lips.

"It's jist us noo Mary, you an' me an' Ah'll gie ye a good life, Ah promise ye."

"Aye, Ah know ye will Johnny, yer a guid man an' Ah'll be a guid wife tae ye."

Together they lay in the long grass by the banks of the River Clyde and under the warm afternoon sun Johnny made Mary his wife. Later as they made their way back to join the festivities, they could hear the fiddles and accordions and the sounds of the dancer's feet on the boards. The crowd cheered as they came into the camp and of course there were ribald comments that made Mary blush, but they took it all in good sport and laughed with everyone else.

Johnny pulled his scarf from his pocket and tied it over Mary's eyes to blindfold her.

"Whit ye daein' Johnny?"

"Come wi' me Mary," he said as he led her past the dancers, and everyone stopped what they were doing and followed on. Willie had fetched the new wagon and everyone had, at one time or another, unbeknown to Mary, filled it with everything that she would need to give her a good start. Johnny stopped Mary in front of her new home and removed her blindfold to reveal the dark green bow topped wagon. All the woodwork was highly varnished and decorated with hand carved scroll. Two brass Tilly lamps hung either side at the front and there were steps at the back for access. Struts fixed under the wagon would allow them to carry or store whatever they needed and various pots jugs and even a galvi bath hung on the sides.

Mary put her hands over her face and cried. This was beyond her expectations and everyone had been so good to her. She was overwhelmed and she felt guilty because she could have been nicer to many of those who had given her these gifts.

"It's too much, Ah didnae expect a' this, Ah don't know how tae thank everybody."

Everyone was touched and pleased to see Mary showing her emotions and most felt that this could be a turning point in her life, and it was, for a while anyway.

Mary and Johnny ran back to Isabella's and untied their cords, quickly retying them as soon as she changed into her red dress. It had a wide skirt, nipped in at the waist, and trimmed with the hematite beads that she had sewn around the edge of the neckline. She had added an extra tier of material to the bottom making the skirt full, so that it would spin out for dancing. The skirts flounced as she walked showing the black lace that she had attached just under the hem, and the effect was stunning. She had new black shoes with a small block heel perfect for dancing, and she had added red ribbon to lace them up.

Everyone was in the middle of the camp, when Mary and Johnny joined them to a rousing cheer. The fiddles and accordions resumed and everyone toasted the happy couple's health. Someone called out to Johnny "Sing us a song Johnny," others joined in, "Aye Johnny, sing us a song."

Johnny sat where he was on a wooden box, his father Willie sat by him with his fiddle tucked under his chin, Johnny took a breath and began to sing in a beautiful baritone…

'Johnny was born in a mansion doon in the county o' Clare

Rosie was born by a roadside somewhere in County Kildare

Destiny brought them together on the road to Killorglan

One day in her bright tasty shawl, she was singing

And she stole his young heart away

for she sang...

Meet me tonight by the campfire

Come with me over the hill.

Let us be married tomorrow

Please let me whisper 'I will'

What if the neighbours are talkin'

Who cares if your friends stop and stare

You'll be proud to be married to Rosie,

Who was reared on the roads of Kildare.

Think of the parents who reared ye

Think of the family name

How can you marry a Gypsy?

Oh whit a terrible shame

Parents and friends stop your pleading

Don't worry about my affair

For I've fallen in love with a Gypsy

Who was reared on the roads of Kildare

Johnny went down from his mansion

Just as the sun had gone down

Turning his back on his kinfolk

Likewise, his dear native town

Facing the roads of old Ireland

With a Gypsy he loved so sincere

When he came to the light of the campfire

These are the words he did hear

Meet me tonight by the campfire

Come with me over the hill.

Let us be married tomorrow

Please let me whisper 'I will'

What if the neighbours are talkin?

Who cares if yer friends stop and stare

You'll be proud to be married to Rosie,

Who wus reared on the roads of Kildare.

Mary listened to the words that she had heard many times before, but on this occasion, these words struck a chord and reminded her that her sister had run away. She sat where she was but her eyes filled with tears; she knew that neither Johnny nor Willie meant any offence but it was a sad reminder that her sister wasn't present. When the song ended, everyone clapped and cheered and then Willie stood, walked over to where Mary was sitting and began to play a rousing tune on his fiddle, all the while teasing Mary and giving her the nod that he wanted her to dance. Mary giggled and at first resisted, but Johnny gave her a gentle push and she rose to the occasion. She assumed a taunting pose, with her hands by her sides clutching the skirts of her dress, hitching the sides up a little and looking at Willie. At first, she danced around him, her feet echoing in time to the fiddle. Willie moved to one side and those who had the traditional Celtic drum the bodhran, began to beat out the rhythm, while others joined them tapping the rhythm on the boxes they were sitting on.

Holding her skirts high at the sides now, Mary had the floor and she spun and tapped and taunted and teased, dancing sensuously towards Johnny offering her hand and as he reached out she would spin away laughing at him, looking over her shoulder to tease him and the look she gave him offered more. Those who watched appreciated her dancing skills, and were as amused as she was. Johnny was overwhelmed with love and passion for his sensual bride. Eventually he could stand the taunting no more, and he leapt to his feet and joined her in the dance. Everyone jumped to their feet, cheered and stamped at this exhibition of passion and love between the two.

Chapter 29

Mary was happier than she had ever imagined that she could be. She had a lovely wagon and all the things that she needed. She and Johnny soon fell into a rhythm of working together. Mary would start her day by cleaning the wagon and preparing the food that she would cook later. Johnny would go to the horse field where Mary would join him when she was finished whatever she happened to be doing on that day. When Johnny travelled, Mary was by his side. They were as inseparable as they always had been and there were no teething problems settling in together. All they needed and wanted more than anything was their own baby to love and cherish and make their family complete. Mary often went across to sit with Nellie to chat, and when she did young Eddie would climb up on to her knees.

"Aye, he loves his Auntie Mary," Nellie would often say and Mary would have her face buried in Eddie's neck blowing little kisses on him while he giggled with delight.

"It's been three months, should Ah no" be pregnant already?"

"It disnae aye happen like that Mary, it'll happen when God's willin'," but every month, like clockwork, Mary bled and every time she bled, she cried. Her dearest wish was for a child of her own, a daughter, but Eddie filled this gap in her life.

She was with Johnny tending to the horses when a terrible pain gripped her in her stomach. She doubled over clutching herself and the colour drained from her face.

"Whit's up Mary!" cried Johnny in alarm.

"Ah'm fine, it's jist a pain," and then she collapsed in a heap at his feet.

"Dear God Mary, speak tae me Mary, for God's sake Mary." He gathered her up in his arms and ran as if the devil himself was after him calling all the while "Mither, Mither!" He ran towards his wagon and Isabella appeared and followed him. He laid Mary down on their bed. "Whit's up wi' her, whit's happenin'?"

Isabella ushered him out of the wagon telling him to fetch Nellie. Mary's skirt was wet with blood and Isabella feared the worst was happening.

"Fetch a basin o' hot water an' bring it quick," she called to him.

"Oh my God, whit's happenin," said Nellie as she rushed to her mother's bidding. Hearing the commotion, Daisy arrived and seeing Johnny in a state of distress outside and thinking that one of the horses had kicked Mary asked him, "Whit's up Johnny, has she been kicked?"

"Naw, she jist got a pain and collapsed, Ah'm worried sick."

Some of the others came around too and sat with Johnny and Daisy while Isabella and Nellie tended to Mary. They stripped off her clothes and washed her down but the blood still came.

"Tell Johnny tae fetch the doctor Nellie."

Nellie stuck her head out of the wagon. "Go for the doctor Johnny." Johnny stood there with his mouth open in shock. One of the other lads called, "Stay here Johnny, Ah'll go, whit will Ah say is wrang?"

"Tell him she's bleeding bad."

Johnny was in a state of shock and didn't know what to do. Someone stuck a glass of whisky in his hand and made him drink it. When the glass was drained, he put his head in his hands and moaned, "Dear God, dinnae let me lose her, dinnae let me lose her. Ah could stand jist aboot onythin' but Ah couldnae stand that."

It was an hour or more before the doctor arrived and Isabella stayed in the wagon with him while he examined Mary.

"Ah'm sorry to tell you that you have lost your baby Mary."

"That cannae be, Ah' didnae know Ah' was pregnant, Ah never missed."

"Sometimes that happens Mary, never mind, there will be other chances."

Mary began to cry and her mind raced. *'Ah was pregnant an' Ah didnae know, maybe Ah did summat Ah shouldnae have done.'*' She was inconsolable.

"She needs to rest her body now and take things easy for a few weeks and then she can try again," the doctor said to Isabella before he left. He nodded to Johnny who was standing at the bottom of the steps waiting. "Whit's wrang wi' her Doctor?"

"I'm afraid that she has lost her baby but she will be fine now, plenty of rest for a few weeks and then she can try again."

"A baby!"

"A very early pregnancy, now if you'll excuse me," he said and hurried off leaving Johnny dismayed.

Isabella came down the steps, "Ye can go in an' see her now, but she's upset."

He went into the wagon, knelt beside the bed, and put his arms around Mary who was crying quietly. Seeing Johnny set her off again and she wept loudly "Oh Johnny wi' made a baby an' now it's gone Ah'm so sorry."

"Ma darlin', hush now, hush, don't upset yer self," but Johnny cried with her as he thought of the baby that might have been.

Isabella went to her wagon, and searched until she found what she was looking for, a paper bag containing red raspberry leaves. She took them across to Mary and Johnny. "Every morning make a pot of tea wi' a spoonful o' these leaves Johnny and gie it tae Mary tae sup. Two or three times a day ye need tae drink this Mary an' it'll help ye get back tae normal. Mind Johnny, a fresh pot every day an' make sure she drinks it." Then to Mary she said as she was leaving, "Ye'll be fine lass, ye'll have bairns."

Mary struggled to come to terms with her grief and this slowed the healing process. She was prone to bouts of weeping without knowing that she was even going to cry. It was as though she had no control of her emotions. Everyone did their best to spend time with her, trying to console her but losing her father and then her sister and now a baby was just too much for her to bear. Gradually, with everyone's love and support, she began to recover and soon it became just another hurt buried deep in her heart. As much as she wanted to be around Johnny, helping with the horses, he was afraid to let her lift or carry anything in case she damaged herself so she gave up trying. Instead, she spent her time with Nellie, and young Eddie, who was growing fast, would climb on to her knee and take her mind off her worries.

"For a lassie that didnae have any wee brothers or sisters yer good wi' the wean."

"Och Nellie, he's a wee soul an easy tae mind."

"Dinnae you worry Mary, ye'll have yer ane afore long."

Winter came and went and, soon enough, spring was beginning to show signs of arriving. Mary finally appeared to be back to her normal self and Johnny felt relieved and happy, but no sooner were they getting used to things being normal when it happened again and it was the same as before. No hint of morning sickness, no hint of missed cycles, nothing. Nothing at all told her that she was once more with child until the pain doubled her in two, and the blood that poured from her stained her clothes.

She was with Isabella when it happened. "Dear God! No' again!" said Isabella when she saw the blood. Isabella sent for Johnny and together they helped Mary to their wagon. Once more, the doctor came and when he had seen to Mary, he took Johnny aside.

"Bring her into the hospital tomorrow morning; she will need a small operation. It's nothing to worry about."

"Whit kind o' operation Doctor?"

"We need to make sure that everything is cleared away and we can have a better look at what has caused her to miss-carry again. You will be able to wait and bring her home but she must have bed rest for at least a week and wait six weeks before you, well before you and she, you know…"

Johnny was worried sick, but he did his best to play down his concerns as he told Mary where she was going. He expected a reaction but Mary just lay there quietly and didn't say a word. The next day Johnny helped Mary into the cart for the journey to the Glasgow Royal Infirmary.

Chapter 30

Mary was like a shadow of her former self in those first few weeks after losing her second baby. She had lost weight and her skin was too pale with dark circles under her eyes. She didn't speak to anyone unless she was spoken to and she avoided others wherever and whenever she could. She would peek out of her wagon and wait until no one was around before venturing out. Both Nellie and Daisy tried to comfort her but she refused to say a word. Johnny was at a loss and didn't know what to do for the best. Everyone was worried about her.

About seven weeks after her hospital visit Mary finally broke; in the middle of the night while everyone slept, Mary slipped out of bed and left Johnny asleep in their wagon. She had no real plan in mind, she didn't know where she was going or why, she just wandered away from the camp. The full moon meant that she could see clearly ahead of her as she began to walk through the trees towards the River Clyde, not stopping until she reached her favourite spot. In her mind, she cursed; she cursed her life, she cursed the Lady in the Moon, she cursed her body, and finally she dropped to the ground, a silent scream escaping her lips. The pain in her spirit was as real as any pain she had physically so far suffered. She pounded the ground in a rage at her loss and cried herself into an exhausted sleep.

Johnny awoke early just as the sun was breaking and realised that Mary wasn't beside him. He quickly pulled on his shirt and trousers and left the wagon. He went over to the dunny first hoping that she would be there but there was no sign of her. All the wagons were set in a semi circle so it was easy for him to see, but there was no sign of her around any of the wagons either. He went to the horse field thinking that she must be there, she wasn't. He took off through the trees, running now, afraid of what he might find, or worse not find.

Mary was lying in the grass, her clothes wet with morning dew, her hair wild from running her hands through it, and her skin pale and almost transparent. At first, he thought she was dead but she stirred as he ran to her and gathered her in his arms.

"Ah' jist want tae die Johnny, Ah've failed ye an' Ah've failed ma bairns. Ah couldnae haud on tae them."

Johnny tried to console her, "It's a' ma fault, it's 'cause Ah've been bad."

"Whit dae ye mean, how can ye say that?"

"The old Mither told me long ago that if Ah did bad things then bad would come back tae me."

Nerves made Johnny want to laugh almost with relief at the absurd claim but he knew better. "Whit bad things dae ye think ye've done?"

"Ah've been angry an' hurt people's feelin's, Ah helped ma sister tae run away wi' Robert an' it finished ma Da. Ah killed ma Da tae!"

"Mary, Mary, ye didnae kill yer Da, he drank himself tae death an' ye didnae make yer sister run away, she did that herself an' its' no' yer fault. Yer jist sufferin' 'cause ye have lost yer bairns but the doctor said ye can have others." He held her for a while then took his hankie from his trouser pocket and soaked it in the river. He gently wiped her face with the cool wet cloth. "Come on Mary, let's get ye back tae the wagon." He helped her up and together they went back to the camp. Johnny made her some tea and settled her into bed. "Sleep now lass, ye need rest tae get ye better." He sat with her for a while until she slept and then he went across to Isabella.

"She's grievin' bad Mither an' Ah dinnae ken whit tae dae."

Isabella reached across and placed a comforting hand over his. "There's nothin' ye can dae Johnny, it's jist time she needs tae heal. Lovin' her an' takin' care o' her the way ye dae is a' she needs an' before ye know it she'll be back on her feet."

"She has it in her mind that she is bein' punished for bein' bad."

"Whit!"

"The old Mither told her if she did owt bad it would come back tae her."

"Oh Johnny Ah remember that from when she was a wee lassie wi' an awfy temper but Ah dinnae think that has owt tae dae wi' whit's happenin'."
"She thinks it's her fault that Coralina ran away or at least it's her fault for helpin' her and she's blamin' hersel' for her Da dyin'. She thinks that's why the bairns came away."

"Mither of God!"

"Ah ken, how dae Ah deal wi' that?"

"Whit did ye say tae her?"

"Ah told her it's no' her fault, but Ah dinnae think it made a difference, She's sleepin' noo, I expect she'll sleep for a while."

"Well wi' jist need tae keep an eye on her an' dae the best wi' can."

Over the next few months everyone looked out for Mary, they kept her company and made sure that she didn't spend too much time on her own. The arrival of summer helped and as her body recovered so too did her spirit. Young Eddie was a blessing because he was the first one to make Mary laugh and the sound was so unusual that those who heard her turned and looked at her with such feelings of gladness that for some it brought tears to their eyes.

No one asked her how she was feeling because that would just remind her of the babies that she had lost. It didn't stop her thinking of them though, they were always in her mind. Johnny began to recover too for he had been in such an anxious state, every bit as sad about his lost children, but more concerned about Mary, and worried about how this would affect them in the future.

By the end of the summer, Mary was almost back to normal. Her colour had returned and she had gained the weight that she had lost following the miscarriage but her monthly cycle had ceased to be regular sometimes bleeding twice in the month and sometimes missing a month altogether. At first, she was concerned, but after talking to the other women, she was reassured that this sometimes happened.

Chapter 31

It had been a good summer and now that October had arrived, folks in the camp were checking their provisions and making ready for the winter months. Mary had gone on a few trips with Johnny and they had visited the Millers in their new rented cottage. They were happy to hear that Robert and Coralina were doing well, but they didn't mention anything about their loss to the Millers. After they returned from one such visit, Mary complained of feeling sick in her stomach.

"Ah must have ate summat bad," she said after returning from one of many trips to the dunny.

"Ye should lie down Mary," said Johnny, concerned.

"Naw, Ah feel fine, it was jist a wee turn for the worst."

Over the next few weeks, Mary continued to be sick and sometimes her complexion took on an almost grey hue. If she had had eyes on the back of her head, she would have seen the other women watching her and giving each other knowing looks, but when she felt sick, she felt so bad that she couldn't begin to notice what anyone else was doing. She began to lose her appetite and then just as suddenly she would be hungry but each time she put food to her lips she had to run away to be sick again. It got to the stage that she could even keep water down and at that time, Isabella took charge.

"Right Johnny, get the cart. That lassie needs tae go tae the hospital." Johnny was shocked but at the same time almost relieved, that someone was making a decision because he was at his wits end and didn't know what to do. Mary was too sick to her stomach to care so she climbed onto the cart without an objection.

They waited for what seemed like ages in the cold tiled corridor and watched porters, nurses, and auxiliaries hurrying about their business until finally a nurse approached them.

"You can go up and see her now; she is in the maternity ward upstairs on the first floor."

Isabella just nodded, but as she looked at Johnny, she almost laughed, as there was a look of shock on his face. "Does that mean she's pregnant?" he asked in amazement.

"Aye, Ah had a feelin' she was."

Johnny ran ahead, taking the stairs two at a time while Isabella made her way up at a slower pace. He reached the ward and scanned the rows of beds until he saw his Mary. Hurrying to her, he folded her in his arms. She was grinning from ear to ear. "Ah'm gonnae have a bairn and the doctor said Ah'm a'right. He said Ah' have a greedy baby an' that's why they have me on this drip."

"Does it hurt ye Mary?"

"Naw, Ah canny feel it. He said Ah have tae bide here till the morra'."

Isabella came into the ward and over to Mary's bedside, she gave her a hug, "Yer' gonnae have a bairn then?"

"Aye, Ah'm really happy, but Ah'm scared as well, but the doctor said that everythin' should be fine this time. That's why Ah' have been so sick."

They stayed a while with Mary until the nurse came and hurried them away.

"It's good timin' Johnny."

"How dae ye mean?"

"Well she can rest up ower the winter an' the bairn will come in the summer an' that will gie it a guid start tae build some strength afore next winter comes."

"Dae ye think it will be… Ah mean dae ye think she will be able tae carry it?"

"Aye, Ah have a guid feelin aboot this wan Johnny, it's been different, she was never sick afore. Ah' think she's carryin' this wan right."

Isabella was right, Johnny brought Mary home from the hospital and from that day, she bloomed as her stomach swelled. Every day she wore a happy smile on her face and she did as she was told, she took things easy spending her time between Nellie's, playing with little Eddie, and Isabella's. She was playing with Eddie when her own baby kicked for the first time. She stopped suddenly and looked at Eddie who looked back at her and then she looked at Nellie who was aware of the sudden change.

"Whit's up Mary?"

"Ah felt it, it kicked me, an' Ah think it kicked Eddie tae," she laughed, "Look at his wee face. Did ye feel the wee baby?" Eddie was just two years old, too young to understand but it was as though he did when he placed his little hand on Mary's bump.

"The wee soul, Ah think he kens," laughed Mary.

The winter came and it was cold and miserable but with every day that passed Mary grew more content and happy. Both she and Johnny were thrilled at the prospect of having their own child. By the time spring came Mary was heavy with child and waddled rather than walked. The baby was due to arrive in May, until then, she passed her time visiting, chatting, and sometimes going to stand by the horses' field to stroke Mizzie and give her a treat. When Johnny went to fetch provisions or sell horses Mary stayed at home. When the moon was full, she would walk through the trees and standing by her favourite spot, she would give thanks to the Lady in the Moon for her blessings and pray for a safe delivery of her baby. When any of the others went off to visit fairs, she and Johnny stayed behind. He didn't want to take her in case anything went wrong but he didn't want to go and leave her behind.

One night she woke, feeling uncomfortable because of pains in her back and Johnny heard the creak of the steps as she left the wagon.

"Mary! Whit's up?"

"Nuthin' Johnny, ma backs jist a wee bit sore an' Ah canny get comfortable."

He pulled on his trousers and went out to join her. "Ah'll make ye a cup o' tea."

"Aye, that would be nice Johnny." Johnny was stoking the fire under the big kettle when Mary got up from the box that she was sitting on.

"Whit ye daein'."

"Ah think Ah need tae pee, Ah'm goin' tae the dunny, oops, too late Johnny, Ah' think Ah've wet ma self'." When Johnny looked over at her, she was bent over, laughing at herself, but Johnny knew what was happening. He dropped the cup he was holding, turned, and ran to Isabella's wagon. George was the first to rouse.

"Whit's's up, whit's the ruckus?"

"Wake Isabella, Ah think Mary's started." He ran back across the short distance to find Mary leaning over against the side of their wagon, both her hands braced on the wooden rim. When she turned to look at him he knew that she was in labour, her face pinched with pain. "Dae ye think its ma time Johnny?"

"Aye, let's get ye up the steps an' on the bed."

By the time Isabella had thrown on her clothes, Nellie and Daisy were up too, as well as some of the other women. Everyone was hurrying about filling the big kettle, tearing up cloths, and generally making things ready for the arrival of the new baby. Johnny sat outside the wagon with the men and some of the women. By morning, there was still no sign of the baby. Nellie and Daisy were whispering to each other praying that everything would be all right. "Ah think it's takin' too long Daisy." Just as they were speaking, Isabella came out of the wagon and summoned George, "Away for the doctor George, jist tae be safe."

Johnny jumped to his feet "Whit's up? Has summat' happened?"

"Naw Johnny, she's jist worn oot an' the bairn is takin' its time, better tae be safe than sorry."

"Can Ah be wi' her?"

"No' the noo Johnny jist bide where ye are." It was some time before the doctor arrived and he went straight into the wagon. Another hour passed and eventually they all heard loud lusty cries of the newborn baby.

Impatient, Johnny said, "For God's sake whit's keeping them?" No one said anything in return, they all waited silently now for someone to appear and reassure them that all was well; and Isabella did.

"It's a lovely wee lassie, well she's no' so wee, she's an eight pounder."

"Whit aboot Mary?" asked Johnny.

"Aye Mary's fine, she's worn out an' she's lost a lot o' blood but she'll be fine."

Someone produced a bottle of whisky, and everyone toasted Mary, Johnny, and the new arrival. After what seemed like a long time, the doctor came out and took Johnny to one side. "Mary and your wee girl will be fine but she will need a good few weeks to recover from this birth. There has been a bit of damage, she's lost a lot of blood, and I'm sorry to say that it's unlikely that there will be any more babies."

Johnny thanked the doctor and tentatively went into the wagon. His heart was overwhelmed with love and joy, with tears streaming down his face as he looked at his Mary and his tiny daughter cradled in her arms. He knelt beside the bed and he kissed Mary on her lips and then gently kissed his little girl.

"She's bonny Mary an' she's got rosy cheeks," he said as he gently drew a finger over the sleeping babies cheek, "an' look at her wee lips, she's like a wee rose bud. Whit are we gonnae call her?"

Mary was smiling as she answered, “Rosa, oor wee rose bud.”

“Can Ah pick her up?”

Mary handed Rosa to her father, he held her close gazing into her eyes and gently stroked her tiny hand, and then the magic happened, as it always does when a grown man finds that moment of pure love that he feels for his newborn child, and Rosa clutched his finger. Eddie looked at Mary, his eyes wide with wonder, “She’s holdin’ ma finger Mary, look,” and they both cried tears of joy.

Chapter 32

That was a beautiful summer; Mary took her time resting, nursing Rosa, and building up her strength, while Nellie and Daisy took on some of her chores. Most days she sat in the sun enjoying her baby and being amused by little Eddie's reactions to Rose. The first time he saw Rosa, his little eyes lit up with amazement, he stretched over and kissed her on the lips. Mary and Daisy laughed as Nellie said, "Aye there's a match made in heaven." From that day, Eddie was never very far from Mary. Rosa fascinated him, and he watched over her even while she slept. Johnny was so proud of his little family and he was happy that Mary was recovering well enough to venture out on the cart for short trips. He liked showing off his family and was keen to do so as often as possible. Mary had taken to motherhood easily, enjoying every moment that she spent with Rosa, and Rosa was a good baby even when she began teething. She seldom cried and she slept through the night.

"Aye, ye've got it easy wi' that bairn Mary, Ah dinnae think Ah've heard her cryin', she's a wee gem, so even tempered," said Nellie.

"She takes after her Da, Ah don't think she has ma nature."

"Well Ah didnae want tae say that ma self but Ah think ye might be right," replied Nellie laughing.

Mary didn't take any offence at the reference to her younger days.

"Ah wanted tae ask ye summat?"

"Whit?"

"Dae ye still see stuff?"

"Aye, but Ah've learned tae keep ma mouth shut."

"Does it jist happen or can ye make it happen?"

"Sometimes it jist happens an' sometimes Ah can make it happen, why dae ye ask?"

"Well Ah ken ye tell fortunes when ye go aroon the doors, but is that for real or dae ye jist make it up?"

"Ah dinnae make it up!" exclaimed Mary. "An' Ah wonder why yer askin me?"

"It's oor Daisy, she's fair love sick, she likes a fella that she sees at the fairs. Could ye see summat for her?"

Mary laughed, "Aye, Ah could, tell her tae come an' have a drink o' tea an' Ah'll read her. Wait till Rosa's settled for the night."

"Thanks Mary, she'll be glad o' that, she's been on at me tae ask ye."

Nellie was quiet for a bit, obviously mulling over something else that she wanted to say.

"Mary, can Ah ask ye how ye dae that, Ah mean how dae ye see things, Ah mean whit's it like?"

"It jist comes, ye ken, like it's happenin' an' Ah can see it clear, other times its jist a feelin'."

"Di's it happen aw' the time?"

"Naw, that would drive ye crazy," said Mary laughing.

"Can ye dae it whenever ye want?"

"Ah suppose Ah can."

"Can ye see onythin' aboot me?"

"Have ye got a sixpence?" said Mary laughing at her own joke. "Ah'm only kiddin', Ah didnae need yer sixpence."

"Well whit dae ye see?"

"Ye've nuthin' tae worry aboot, but Ah'll miss ye when ye go."

Nellie startled, jumped in her seat, "Whit dae ye mean? Am Ah' gonnae die?"

"Don't be stupid, Ah didnae mean that yer gonnae die Ah meant when ye go somewhere else."

"Where am Ah goin'?"

"Ah'll tell ye after Ah read Daisy's tea leaves."

"So Ah'm a'right then?"

"Aye, yer fine," laughed Mary.

"Dae ye ever see owt bad?"

"Aye, sometimes, but Ah dinnae aye ken whit it means 'cause sometimes its jist a really bad feelin' and Ah dinnae ken whit's gonnae happen'."

"Ah widnae like that."

"Sometimes Ah dinnae like it either."

Later that evening Daisy and Nellie joined Mary and the three of them sat on boxes outside Mary's wagon, each with a cup of hot tea. They were chatting normally, but there was an undercurrent of anticipation, especially from Daisy. Although they had settled their differences just before Mary's wedding, Mary was still closer to Nellie, and Daisy still hadn't achieved the familiarity with Mary that Nellie had with her.

"Are ye done huggin' that cup Daisy?"

"Aye, here."

"That's nae use, ye still have a drop o' tea in the bottom, sup it till its dry." Daisy pursed her lips together to prevent the tealeaves from getting into her mouth and then she gave the cup back to Mary. They sat quietly for a few moments while Mary studied the leaves.

"Whit can ye see?" asked Daisy.

"Wheesht, Ah'm readin' it." After a few moments more, Mary began to speak. "Right the first thing is somebody is gonnae bring ye some news, an' there's a big crowd. There's a lot o' flowers in yer cup tae and that's compliments an' nice things happenin'..."

"Dae ye mean it's ma weddin'?"

"Naw, it's no', there's a journey either side o' it so it looks as though ye go somewhere an' there's a lot of people and then ye come back. Then there's another journey further on. That journey will come after yer ain weddin. Ye'll no' stay here an' ye'll take Nellie wi' ye..."

"Whit dae ye mean, she'll take me wi' her?"

"Two lassies, two men an' young Eddie as well."

"Ah'm no' gone anywhere."

"The leaves say different."

"Where am Ah goin, an' when?" exclaimed Nellie.

"Ah told ye, sometime after her weddin'."

"Who am Ah getting' wed tae?" interrupted Daisy.

"Ah cannae tell ye that, but he has ginger hair."

Daisy gasped, "It's him, it must be him, he's got ginger hair."

"Who has?" asked Mary.

"The fella she's sweet on, Bruce, he's no' fae aboot here, he's fae Carlisle," said Nellie. "He's a Donnelly, ye see him at Appleby an' the like."

Mary's prediction came true later that summer, when they all went to Appleby fair, and Bruce asked George if he could have Daisy's hand in marriage. She was beside herself with excitement and couldn't wait to share her news with Mary.

"Ah'm getting' wed Mary! Ye were right, Bruce asked ma Da for ma hand an' he said aye. Ah'm so happy."

Mary hugged Daisy, "Ah'm right pleased for ye Daisy, when is it tae happen?"

"At the end o' the summer, when the harvest is in. Ah want tae get wed in the camp wi' ma Da daein' ma vows."

"He's right clever, he makes an fixes wheels for carts, an' he's got plans for the future."

Mary knew this to be true and she knew that this would bring about the next part of her prediction, the part that she was less pleased about because that would take Nellie, Edward and young Eddie away to live somewhere else and she knew that she would miss them very much.

It was a lovely sunny October day when Daisy and Bruce got married and the celebrations went on long into the night. Mary and Johnny were back in their wagon when Johnny asked Mary why she looked so sad.

"Ah'm gonnae miss seein' Nellie an' wee Eddie when they go."

"Dae ye no' mean Daisy?"

"Aye, she's goin' as well, but Nellie an' Eddie will go tae?"

"Who told ye that?"

Mary just raised her eyes and looked at Johnny for a minute and then she said, "Ah've seen it, and they'll be away afore the snow comes."

"Och maybe yer mistaken,"

"Ah'm never mistaken Johnny, an' am surprised that ye would say that."

"Perhaps yer right then." Johnny knew that if Mary had seen it then there was a good chance that it would happen, but he would miss Edward if he left.

Isabella was heartbroken when Daisy and Bruce left to settle in a camp in Carlisle where the Donnelly's lived. George had a tear in his eye as his youngest daughter left with her new husband, but there were more tears to follow only they did not know that yet.

Chapter 33

Isabella and George were sitting in their wagon one evening not long after Daisy and Bruce had left to begin their new life in Carlisle when Edward and Nellie came across to visit with little Eddie. They sat chatting for a while but Isabella had the feeling that something was coming, but she wasn't sure what. Eventually Edward broached the subject that had been hanging in the air. "Bruce has got a guid thing goin' in Carlisle."

George and Isabella both looked over at him waiting for more and Isabella glanced at Nellie who was biting her bottom lip, a sure sign that she was worried about what was to come next.

"Whit's that?" answered George.

"Well ye ken he's a wheelwright."

"Aye."

"Well wi' were talkin' an' he has plans tae build wagon's an' he asked me if Ah wanted tae go in wi' him. He would dae the wheels an' frames for the wagons an' Ah could dae the insides. Ah could make a guid job o' that."

"Aye, Ah'm sure you could," replied George cautiously, knowing there was more to come.

"Thing is, it would mean me an' Nellie an' wee Eddie movin' tae Carlisle."

Isabella put her hands to her mouth and her eyes began to fill with tears.

Nellie rushed over to kneel in front of her mother, "Oh' Mam, dinnae greet, it's no' that far away an' wi'll see ye from time tae time."

"So how come ye cannae dae this here? Bruce could come here," replied George.

"Aye he could but he's established in Carlisle and that's where o' the business is these days. He's getting a lot o' work fae the borders an' the North o' England."

George sat quietly for a few minutes and then he replied, "Aye, Ah suppose yer right it does make sense, but Ah'll be sorry tae see ye go. When are ye thinkin' o' leavin'?"

Isabella gasped as Edward replied, "This week."

Nellie was still kneeling in front of her mother, but now she was crying silent tears. "Oh' Mam Ah'll miss ye tae."

Everything appeared to have changed and the change had crept quietly up on everyone. The last part of Mary's prediction had come true. Daisy and Bruce along with Nellie, Edward and young Eddie had gone to Carlisle. Johnny missed Edward's company and Mary particularly missed Nellie, but she had Rosa to take her attention and she spent much of her spare time keeping Isabella company because she was sad not having her daughters nearby.

All too soon, summer ended and by the end of October, the winter had come in with a bang, one storm after another, and rain for days on end. Johnny was patiently waiting for a break in the weather so that he could make the last trip for their winter supplies. He had put off going until after Daisy and Bruce's wedding, and then he put it off again to wish Nellie and Edward well when they were leaving for Carlisle. When the rain finally stopped,

Johnny was reluctant to leave, because Rosa, who was now five months old, had developed a bad cold but Mary thought that it would pass in a few days. She had a bad feeling about it but convinced herself that it was just because she was a mother now, and a mother always worries. Johnny kissed them both before leaving and promised to be back the next day but he had no sooner gone than it started to snow.

Isabella had gone over to Mary's wagon to see how the little one was. Rosa's face was flushed red, her nose was blocked, and she had started to cough. Mary had done everything that she could think of. Isabella suggested trying steam to ease her breathing so she fetched a pot of hot water and placed it on the table. Mary sat beside the table with Rosa in her arms and Isabella placed a sheet over them both so that the steam from the pot would stay under the sheet. This didn't appear to make much difference and Mary could stand it no longer, she was afraid for her daughter.

"Ah'm gonnae take her tae the Royal."

"Ye cannae dae that yer self, a' the men are away, whit ye gonnae dae, walk!"

"Ah'm gonnae run," said Mary and she quickly grabbed a big woollen blanket and wrapped her and Rosa up in it.

"Ye cannae go yer self whit if ye fa' wi' the wean? Its slippy oot there. Ah'll come wi' ye."

"Ye'll need tae keep up wi' me Isabella for Ah huvnae any time tae wait for ye."

At that, Isabella ran to her wagon, and quickly grabbed her warm shawl and head scarf then ran as best she could to catch up with Mary. It had only been seconds since she left Mary but the snow was falling so fast now that she could hardly see her ahead. "Ah'm comin, Mary," she called. Mary was just a dark silhouette on that path. They cut through Glasgow Green making their way to the Royal Infirmary. The going was treacherous and they could hardly see in front of them.

"Wi'll cut up to London Road," said Mary. Isabella was too busy trying to keep upright to answer and she was worried about Rosa. On and on they tramped, through the thick snow finally reaching London Road. They were exhausted but didn't care. All they could think of was getting Rosa to the hospital. Suddenly they heard the sound of horses pulling a carriage. The snow was a little clearer but still falling thick. They stopped for a moment thinking that they could get help and as the carriage neared them the coachman reigned in the horses, startled by the sudden appearance of the two women, neighed their displeasure and stamped the ground.

"Help me tae get tae the hospital!" cried Mary.

At that, a wealthy looking man pulled down the window at the side of the carriage and looked down at Mary and Isabella. He stared at them.

"Mister, can ye help me tae get tae the hospital?"

Mary could see a gold ring on his finger. "Can ye help me wi' ma wean mister?" The Coachman was leaning over the side watching for his response. The passenger stuck his finger in the air and made a circular gesture, there was a pause for a moment as the coachman looked at the passenger and the passenger said in a loud voice "Drive on." The coachman paused and tried to explain but the man yelled at him in an American accent. "You have been told coachman, drive on."

The coachman looked down at Mary, shook his head sadly, and then did as he was bid. Mary screamed at the American "Naw, naw ye cannae dae that, ma bairns sick!" but she was speaking to the back of the carriage as it pulled away. Rage enveloped her as she ran after the wagon screaming at the top of her voice.

"Ye saw me runnin' in the dark

An' didnae stop an' didnae park

She was sick ma precious bairn

Ah widnae dae ye any hairm.

Ye think ye are an important maister

Yer nothin but a selfish baistard

Tae you an' yours a send Ah curse

Let bad things happen and then the wurst.

Son or daughter from this day on

They'll suffer for yer deeds e'en when yer gone

Ah send this curse just wait an' see

For ye widnae stop an' help ma wane an' me."

The last of her words were called into the snow for she could not see the carriage any more, but she could hear it and with every ounce of her being, she wished ill on the man in the carriage. Mary's words shocked Isabella, cold as she was these words chilled her in a different way, and they would be remembered for a long, long, time. The visit to the hospital was a short one, Rosa was immediately put on oxygen and kept in overnight while Mary and Isabella waited in the cold hospital corridor. By morning, Rosa was much better and although the hospital wanted Isabella and Mary to leave, they wouldn't go without Rosa. After some insistence, they allowed them to take Rosa home. The sky was bright blue, the sun was shining, and there was not a cloud in sight when the little group left the Royal Infirmary that morning. Mary stopped at the doorway and looked up for a few minutes and then she turned to Isabella and said, "Let's get hame Isabella, it'll be a'right noo."

Chapter 34

Johnny was shocked to hear how sick Rosa had been and dismayed to hear that Mary and Isabella had made their way through the blizzard to the hospital. Mary told Johnny about the wealthy American.

"The coachman wanted tae help but the Yankee widnae let him. Ah was ragin', but he'll get whit's coming tae him for no' stoppin' 'cause Ah cursed him wi' a' ma might."

"Mary, Ah've seen ye cryin' yer eyes oot for daein stuff like that. Ah thought ye had learned yer lesson fae old Mither Morrison. Ye told me yer self whit goes aroon comes aroon, Ah wish ye didnae dae that."

"Well it's done noo an' he deserves whit's comin', Ah cannae take it back." Johnny shook his head sadly because he was worried about what might come back. He didn't want something bad to happen to either of them or especially to Rosa who he loved more than he could have imagined.

News of Mary and Isabella' late night dash to the hospital travelled around the camp and at the same time so did the story of the curse that she yelled to the wealthy American. Reading newspapers was not common among the Gypsies for at that time, most of them couldn't read, but that did not stop news travelling. There were always travellers coming and going, some would come from other camps and they would just be passing on their way to another town or village. Often they would take the opportunity to stop for a night or two, and share news and titbits from their own camp or whatever they heard on the way. Likewise, they would carry stories back when they returned home, so it wasn't long before Mary's curse became common knowledge. Some just laughed when they heard of it but others would shiver and shake their head.

The following year the story of the curse raised it head again when Edward, Nellie, and young Eddie came to visit Isabella. They had already spent the day going round the camp, saying hello to old friends and family. Nellie took Eddie across to see Mary and was delighted that Rosa was now toddling about, confident on her feet. Rosa stood and stared at Eddie who was nearly five years old now and then she grinned and put out her arms and in her baby voice, she said, "Up." Everyone laughed including Eddie as he struggled to lift her.

"Ah think she remembers him, Ah told ye that was a match made in Heaven," said Nellie. They went outside with the children so that they could play in the summer sunshine and for a while, they watched fascinated as Eddie and Rosa sat in the sun enjoying each other's company. Eddie took Rosa's hand and wandered round the camp with her grinning from ear to ear. "He loves that wean," said Nellie.

"Ah think yer right."

Nellie didn't share the story, she had been keeping it from Mary, but she was anxious to share it with her mother. Much later when the opportunity arose and she was sitting chatting with Isabella she asked, "Dae ye remember when Mary cursed the Yankee Mam?"

"Aye, whit of it? Ah dinnae like tae remember that."

"Edward came hame wi' a story about a Yankee politician that had spent time in Scotland and there was news that he lost his wean, a wee lad."

"Never!"

"Aye, for sure. There was some talk that a Gypsy had cursed him an' noo he's lost his son. They say it was in the newspapers."

"Oh that's terrible, it cannae be true."

"That's whit Ah'm hearin' Mam."

"Have ye told Mary?"

"Naw, are ye jokin' Ah couldnae tell her that. Ah'm sure she meant it at the time, but Ah think she would be fair heartbroken tae think a wee laddie had died because of it."

"Well maybe he was sick, maybe it wisnae the curse."

"Well that's whit they're sayin' in the camps an' on the road."

"Ah dinnae think ye should mention it tae her."

"Naw Mam, no' me Ah'm no' tellin' her o' it."

"Naw Ah dinnae think ye should for it would only worry her an' their life is sweet. Ah wouldnae like tae see summat bad comin' back tae hurt her, an' Ah widnae like tae see her worryin' that it could."

In spite of Nellie and Isabella trying to keep this gossip from Mary, Edward mentioned it to Johnny.

"Heavens above, dae ye think it's true?"

"Well who can say if it's true or no', but Ah thought it would be better if ye knew aboot it."

"Aye yer probably right Edward, Ah have tae think aboot this, Ah dinnae ken if Ah should tell Mary."

Johnny worried about the story he had heard and Mary sensed that something was troubling him. One evening a few days after Nellie and Edward had left, they were sitting in their wagon. All was quiet, and Rosa was fast asleep.

"Are ye a' right Johnny?"

"Aye, why dae ye ask?"

"It seems tae me that there's summat troublin' ye the past few days."

Johnny made no response and this just confirmed Mary's fears.

"Can ye tell me whit's troublin' ye Johnny?"

"Ah didnae want tae worry ye, but Ah think that there is summat ye should know." Mary was more worried now.

"Tell me Johnny, for ma worry will be greater if ye dinnae say whit it is."

"Ah'll tell ye this Mary, but Ah'm only tellin' ye so that ye can dae summat if it's possible."

Mary sat with bated breath waiting to hear what he had to say. "Dae ye remember the night ye had tae rush tae the hospital wi' Rosa?"

"Aye Ah remember it, Ah'll never forget it as long as Ah live."

"Dae ye remember the Yank that widnae help ye an' ye cursed him?"

"Ah dae."

"They say he's a Yankee Politician."

"Whit of it?"

"They say he had a wee lad an' he has died. They're sayin it was a curse on him by a Gypsy."

"Och that's jist rubbish! How could onybody know that?"

"Ye know how stories get passed Mary. The coachman tells the stable lad, the stable lad tells the housemaids, before ye know it everybody knows. Noo they're saying it was in the papers that he thinks the Gypsy's curse was tae blame for his bairns death."

Mary was quiet, thinking about that night, trying to understand her feelings. She questioned herself, deep in her heart she could not forgive the Yankee, but at the same time she realised that what she had done, the power of the words that she had uttered could have been the cause of the death of a child. She was horrified.

"Dae ye hate me for what Ah said Johnny?"

"Ah could never hate ye Mary but sometimes Ah question yer thinkin'."

All was quiet in the wagon as both of them sat and thought about that night. Johnny wished that he had never made the decision to leave that day. If he had waited another day or two, he could have taken Mary and Rosa to the hospital in the cart and they would never have met the Yankee. Mary's thoughts were on her terror at the thought of losing Rosa and then suddenly, in her mind, she heard old Mither Morrison's voice,

"When ye dae summat bad, the ripples keep movin' until they come back tae ye. Ye ' can dae guid wi' yer gift, but ye can dae harm tae. Dae guid an' guid things will aye come tae ye, but be sure o' this Mary, if ye dae summat bad it's the hardest thing tae take back, and bad will come right back at ye when ye least expect it."

Mary sat there, Mither Morrison's words ringing in her ears and fear of the consequences churning in her stomach. She tried to put a brave face on and pretend that she wasn't bothered, but she was deeply troubled and she realised that she felt guilty that a child had suffered.

Chapter 35

Mary felt sick to her stomach, she tossed and turned unable to sleep, and every time she closed her eyes, she could hear the words of her curse ringing in her ears. Johnny, lying awake beside her, but pretending he was asleep, felt every twist and turn. He was unable to offer any solace to his troubled wife. He was aware of her slipping out of their bed and quietly leaving the wagon. He felt sure that he knew where she was going, her favourite spot by the river. He also knew that on this occasion he should let her be alone. He didn't know what she was going to do, however, he was sure that she would be trying to repair any damage her curse had done.

The moon was waning and instinctively Mary knew that this was a perfect time to ask for something to be sent away. She made her way through the trees and when she reached her favourite spot, she knelt down on the cold damp grass.

"Whit have Ah done, whit have Ah done?" She looked up at the sliver of the Moon and implored,

'Lady of the silver Moon

Help me noo Ah spoke too soon

Ah shed a curse, Ah was feart that night

But noo Ah know Ah wisnae right

Break this curse and make it well

Ah'm awfy sorry, ye can surely tell

Take ma fears an' make things right

Ah beg ye this wi' a' ma might

Ah'm sorry for the curse a made

A curse Ah know Ah shouldnae have said

Take them back Ah beg ye please

Ah'm praying on ma bended knees

Let me an mine aye be well

An listen please tae ma wee spell

Hear me Lady hear me pray

For ne're again a curse Ah'll say."

Mary stayed there for a long time thinking and worrying about what she may have been the cause of, fearing what may happen in the future and then she realised that there was a way she might be able to see ahead. Dawn was breaking as she made her way back through the trees to her wagon. Johnny had the fire going already and water boiled for tea. He saw her approaching, her appearance dishevelled, her dark hair unkempt, her face streaked from crying and her eyes swollen. She walked straight to him and he embraced her and held her in his arms. She was exhausted but sleep was a long way off.

"Dae ye remember that old broken clock ye found Johnny, dae ye know where it is?"

"Here drink this tea, let me have a think, aye, it's in a box under the wagon. Whit dae ye need it for?"

"Jist summat Ah want tae try."

"Ah'll get it for ye."

"Thanks Johnny."

He sat looking at her and was unable to think of what to say to her that would make her feel any better.

"Ah have nae idea how tae help ye Mary."

"There's nothin' ye can say or dae that will make me feel better. Ah've done whit Ah can. Whit Ah did was wrang an' Ah have tae make up for it for the rest o' ma life."

Johnny got up and kissed the top of her head. "Ah'll see if Ah kind find that clock."

Mary heard Rosa stirring as Johnny began to search through boxes that were stored under the wagon. She went in and picked her up smothering her sweet face with kisses. She cried a little too, "Ah'll never let ye oot ma sight ma darlin'."

Rosa, oblivious to her mother's pain, nuzzled into her neck enjoying those first morning moments in her mother's arms.

"Ah've found it Mary."

"Jist leave it there for me Johnny, Ah'll get tae it later."

"Right then Ah'll see ye a bit later, Ah'm away tae see tae the horses."

Mary spent the better part of the morning tending to Rosa's needs and tidying the wagon, later she popped over to see her aunt.

"Yer quiet the day Mary?"

"Aye, Ah've had a rough night."

"Wi' the bairn?"

"Naw Mither, jist summat that's came back tae haunt me."

"Dae ye want tae speak of it?"

"Dae ye remember the night wi' ran tae the hospital wi' Rosa?"

Isabella's breath noticeably hitched and Mary looked at her questioningly.

"Ye've heard the rumours then?"

"Aye Mary, Ah have, but Ah dinnae think ye needed that worry."

"Well it's better that Ah know of it. Maybe Ah can change things."

"Dae ye think ye can?"

"Well Ah've been up a' night tryin' so Ah jist have tae wait an' see."

"Ah'll keep an eye on Rosa if ye want tae go an' have a sleep Mary."

"Thanks Mither but even if Ah lay doon Ah dinnae think Ah could shut ma eyes an' no' see that damage Ah've done. Ah'll be fine, but Ah appreciate the offer."

Later that night Mary took the old clock apart. She had no need of the workings; it was the bevelled glass that she wanted. She searched in her box of trimmings looking for a square of black velvet that she knew she had and then she laid the curved glass on top of it. It was exactly the right size, but she wanted a box to finish her creation. She began to search in the cupboards and cabinets in the wagon and finally she found a wooden box full of buttons and fasteners. She emptied it out putting all the contents to one side; she would find something to keep these treasures in later, but for now the focus of her attention was the box, the black velvet and the curved glass from the old clock.

Later that evening after they had eaten and Rosa was settled for the night Mary spoke to Johnny.

"Ah'm away tae the river Johnny, Ah'll leave ye tae mind Rosa for a wee while."

"Aye lass, she'll be fine wi' me." He stood and kissed her before she left the wagon. "Ah take it ye have a plan?"

"Ah'm gonnae see if Ah can take a look into the future for us."

There was not much that Johnny could say about that because he had no concept of the gifts that Mary had, he just nodded his support.

Mary was careful about gathering all the things that she would need for her task. First into her basket was the box that she had prepared by lining it with the piece of black velvet cloth with the curved glass over it. Next, from her supply of herbs, she added a sprig of Bog Myrtle, a sprig of Rosemary and then from her cupboard she added an earthenware dish, a candle, and finally she placed a cloth to sit on at the top of her basket. On the way to the river, she nipped several leaves from one of the lower branches of an Ash tree. When she arrived at her favourite space, she spread the cloth on the ground and unpacked her basket. She used a stone from the riverbank to grind the Bog Myrtle, the Rosemary and the leaves from the Ash tree earthenware dish. She sat for a few moments to focus her mind on her intention. When she felt that she was ready, she lit her candle and then set the flame to the crushed herbs. Leaning over the smoke from the herbs, she inhaled deeply and used her hand to waft the smoke onto her face. At first, she could feel the smoke making her lightheaded and then the properties began to induce a trance like feeling. She took the wooden box and placed it on her lap so that the light of the moon reflected on it, and then she began to scry in the glass.

At first, she could see nothing but the Moon's reflection but as the effect of the burning herbs began to take effect, pictures began to form. Initially it was almost as though she was seeing through a fine mist but as she concentrated, the pictures became clearer. She wasn't sure of the correct way to do what she was doing but she persevered. She saw Johnny in her vision and he was laughing; she concentrated harder and then she saw Rosa running, laughing with her arms outstretched, and then she saw that Rosa was running to young Eddie. He was laughing too, and he picked her up, swinging her around then put her down and mussed her hair. She saw the whole family at different fairs and Rosa was older and so pretty. She kept looking willing her intention to go as far into the future as she could but the last thing that she saw before she passed out was Eddie handing Rosa a small wooden token carved in the shape of a Rose. She knew in the moment that Rosa and Eddie would marry and she felt a deep sense of contentment.

Chapter 36

Johnny paced about, unable to settle, he was not sure what Mary was actually doing and was feeling useless. Rosa continued to sleep soundly and finally Mary arrived back. Johnny breathed a sigh of relief and clasped her to him.

"Are you a'right Mary?"

"Ah have a really sore head, it's a bad one."

"Ah'll make ye some tea an' then Ah think ye should go tae bed."

Mary drank her tea but she was half asleep before the tea was finished and Johnny took her cup, picked her up in his arms and laid her down to sleep. She slept through the night and late into the morning. When she awoke, Johnny was already away to tend to the horses and Isabella was minding Rosa. "Mither, whit ye daein here, where's Johnny? Is everythin' a'right?"

"It's nearly noon Mary, ye've been asleep for a long while an' Ah've been enjoyin' this wee treasure, here go tae yer Mam," Isabella said, handing Rosa to Mary.

"Ah cannae believe Ah've slept a' that time."

"Johnny was fair worried for ye so Ah came across tae mind the wee one an' let ye sleep."

"Thanks Mither, that was kind o' ye."

"Tis nothin'."

Isabella lifted the teapot that was sitting on top of the Queenie stove, poured a cup of tea, and handed it to Mary. "Drink this lass, an' there's a pancake under the napkin, made fresh this morning. Ye'll feel better wi' summat in yer stomach."

Mary sat with Rosa on her lap, in between bites she gave Rosa little bits of pancake, laughing with Isabella at the happy faces Rosa was making as she enjoyed the treats.

"Johnny said that ye were oot most o' the night trying tae see whit's comin', did ye have any luck?"

"Ah saw a lot o' things Mither, but Ah didnae see owt bad. Ah saw ma bairn growin' aw she was jist beautiful, Ah saw her playin' an' laughin' an' Ah saw her wi' Eddie. Ah think they will wed. He'll make her a fine husband, but after that, it jist got darker an' darker an' Ah couldnae see owt. Ah think maybe Ah fainted, Ah don't think Ah fell asleep an' Ah am no' sure for how long. Ah don't even rightly remember comin back here."

Isabella just nodded. She wasn't sure if this was good or bad, but only time would tell. As it happens, it was just as well that Mary did not see what was coming as the foresight might have killed her. No one could cope with the knowledge of what would happen in times to come, but she didn't see and from that day on life returned to normal for her, Johnny and Rosa.

The whole world was changing around them, not least was the fact that Mary began to call her husband John rather than the Johnny that she had always called him before. By the time Rosa was five years old the first cars were appearing and new opportunities were opening up. People were able to travel farther in a shorter time and there was even some talk of wagons being motorised. Some laughed when they heard and some scorned or scoffed the idea of it. For this camp, everything remained as it had been. Johnny still traded horses and looked after fetching provisions. Mary went along with him and there were often wives waiting to have their fortunes told. They still enjoyed the experience of travelling to fairs and meeting up with their kinfolks and friends and they always looked forward to visits from Nellie and Edward. Eddie was growing fast and he was such a handsome lad and clever too. From an early age, he showed his skills with wood. As soon as Nellie and Eddie would let him handle a sharp knife, he was whittling little bits of wood. Before long, he was making clothes pegs. When he announced that he would sell them round the doors whenever he had made enough of them, Edward and Nellie laughed at his claims, but Eddie was diligent, and before long, his claims became a reality. They didn't laugh when he sold his first batch; in fact, they were very proud of him.

Life goes on as it must do and as time passed Johnny and Mary continued doing what they had always done, breeding, selling, and showing horses. Mary taught Rosa everything that she knew, well almost everything. She taught her how to cook and clean from an early age, and she taught her how to sew on a button or mend a hem, she taught her the benefits of healing herbs, and how to make potions, but she didn't speak to her about spell crafting. When they went to fairs, they met up with Nellie, Edward, and young Eddie and Eddie was always the first to run to them. He missed his Auntie Mary but he missed Rosa more. As soon as they saw each other, they would skip off together holding hands and laughing. From time to time, Nellie, Edward, and young Eddie along with Daisy and Bruce would come back to the camp at Glasgow Green to visit their parents. Those days created special memories for everyone and as always Eddie and Rosa were inseparable.

Rosa had inherited her fathers' temperament and her mother's beauty. From an early age, Eddie's good looks were often the topic of conversation among the young girls wherever he went, but he only had eyes for Rosa. By the time he was twelve years old he was making and selling clothes pegs around the doors and saving for his future. Later he began to construct three legged stools with beautifully turned legs and he sold these as fast as he could make them. Before long, he was carving patterns into the seats and soon he was taking orders, but there was more to Eddie's talent than clothes pegs and stools no matter how pretty the stools were. Often when he was travelling on the cart with his father he would shout to him, "Haud up there Da!" then he would jump down from the cart and run to the edge of the trees where he had spotted a dried up root or a fallen trunk. He could see things in a piece of wood that no one else could, and he could take that wood and spend hours carving out shapes, creating beautiful fruit bowls or plates. He had carved shapes and patterns into the woodwork on his parent's wagon and Nellie delighted in showing off her son's skills.

Eddie was about fourteen years old when, one day, he had just finished carving a bowl when he spotted a small burr of elm that had landed at his feet. Anyone else might have discarded this but Eddie saw something in it immediately. He picked it up and turned it over in his hands, looking at it from all angles and then he sat down and began to carve out the shape that he could see in his mind's eye. First, he smoothed off the edges and when he was satisfied, he began to cut into the surface. He patiently shaped and carved it until it was flat on one side and about two inches across. On the surface, he began to carve the shape that was in his mind. He was engrossed in his project and he had one person in mind during the creation of it, Rosa. When he had finished he once more turned it over and looked at it from all angles and knew, small though it was, it was the finest work he had created. This he created with love in his heart. He carried it in his pocket knowing that the next time he saw Rosa he would give it to her.

Rosa was always excited when they were getting ready to go to any of the fairs, but this wasn't like going to a local fair in Barrhead or Neilston, for they were going to Musselburgh by Edinburgh and they might even get to Portobello beach. She knew that they would meet up with family and friends they hadn't seen but she was more excited at the thought that she would see Eddie again, everyone would be there, especially Eddie.

When they finally arrived at the fair Eddie was watching for them and went to meet their wagon, "Uncle John, Auntie Mary," addressing them as was the custom. He nodded to them but his eyes were for Rosa.

"Can Ah go Da?"

"Ye might ask yer Mam if she needs ye."

"Mam?"

"Away wi' ye Rosa," and then she looked at Johnny and smiled, but he just shook his head. Rosa jumped down from the wagon and ran off with Eddie, both of them laughing and happy to be with each other.

"Ah have summat for ye."

"For me Eddie?"

They were running hand in hand, as they spoke, "Aye."

"Whit is it Eddie?"

"Ye'll see in a minute."

He led her to the edge of the field that the fair was being held in and they both sat on the grass. "Ah've missed ye Rosa, but Ah thought o' ye every day."

Rosa smiled at him still in that early age of awareness but still shy, being with the one she loved, but not truly knowing what that meant yet.

"Gie me yer hand."

Rosa held out her hand and Eddie placed the wooden rose in it. "Ah made this for ye Rosa an' Ah've carried it every day an' Ah would like ye tae keep it tae remind ye o' how Ah feel when we're apart."

Tears filled Rosa's eyes as she looked at it. "It's a rose!"

"Aye, it's a rose for Rosa."

"It's lovely Eddie, Ah will treasure it, an' Ah'll carry it always."

They stayed at the fairground for two days and Rosa and Eddie were together as much as possible, but all too soon, it was time to part.

"Ah don't ken when Ah will see ye next but keep that rose on ye an' think o' me often an' Ah'll be thinkin' o' ye."

Chapter 37

They had managed to get together at several fairs but each time their parting was harder. She would take the wooden rose out of her pocket often, and look at it, treasuring the memories that it evoked and thinking of Eddie. Among her precious things was a box that Eddie had made and given to her at the last fair. It was about eight inches long, four inches wide, and four inches deep. She kept little things in it to remind her of Eddie; inside was a pressed flower, a button from his jacket, and a ribbon that he had bought for her hair. Little things, but looking at them reminded her of him.

Rosa kept her promise and carried the wooden rose in her pocket all the time. The first time Mary saw her looking at her it, she knew exactly where it had come from, but she allowed Rosa her secret and didn't say a word about it. Mary mentioned to John that Eddie had made Rosa a wooden token, "Ah think it's a rose."

"That would be fitting an' Ah'm sure he made a guid job o' it."

She smiled at him as she remembered those first flushes of love.

"Ah will be surprised if they didnae wed each other, they've been stuck like glue since the day she was born."

"Time enough for that Mary. She's only a lassie."

"She's sixteen John, a year or two an' she could be promised tae him an' merried no' long after that."

John didn't want to hear that, acting as most fathers do when they think that their daughter might soon be dependent on someone other than them. "Enough," he said and took himself off to the horses. Mary muttered to herself, "Aye he's got a short memory," shaking her head she continued, "he forgets whit we were like an' Coralina was away wi' Robert by the time she was sixteen." She sighed at the random thought of Coralina and wished her well wherever she was.

It was a fine day and she was intent on washing down all the woodwork on the outside of the wagon. She filled a pail with warm water and then rubbed a cloth in the water with carbolic soap. Her mind drifted back; back to when they were younger, and all the changes that they had experienced since those days. She laughed to herself as she thought of the fight that she had with Daisy just before her wedding, and then she blushed as she remembered her father dragging her from the river like a wild woman. She shook her head trying to rid herself of the embarrassing thought. She thought about Coralina and Robert and wondered how different her life would be if Coralina had loved a Gypsy lad and still lived on the camp. Daisy and Bruce were still in Carlisle with Nellie and Edward; she missed them and was always glad to reunite with them and their children at fairs. Isabella was gone now and so was George and she remembered that they had passed within weeks of each other. It was a shock to everyone, and it still brought a tear to her eye, but it brought Jennie back to the camp with her husband Henry, and their three children, Ellen, Sadie, and Lizzie, it was good to see them back where they belonged.

Before too long she had finished cleaning the wagon, and with everything spick and span she went off to join John at the horse field. Mizzie was gone now too; the bond she had with Mizzie was special and no other horse had touched her heart the way Mizzie had, but she liked them all well enough, and she still had a way with them. They were going to Musselburgh within the next few days and John was making sure that all the horses that he was taking looked their best. Rosa could hardly contain herself because she knew that she would see Eddie and she couldn't think about anything else.

"Are yi takin' some doilies tae sell Rosa?"

"Aye Mam, an' Ah have some wi' nice beads an' shells that Ah think will sell easy."

They had done everything that they needed to do to prepare for the trip and now it was time to leave but Rosa was dithering about, her excitement at seeing Eddie was just too much and she could hardly think straight.

"Hurry Rosa yer Da wants tae leave in ten minutes."

"Ah'm hurryin Ma, Ah'm goin' as fast as Ah can," said Rosa. She hopped about pulling on her black boots and fastening the laces. The last time they had met was at Musselburgh Fair and she couldn't wait to see him again. She was sixteen now, her raven black hair curled and waved over her shoulders and down her back and her green eyes sparkled with excitement.

She turned the wooden rose over and over in her pocket feeling the grooves and shapes that formed the rose. She knew every part of it.

"Hurry up lass," her father called as he hitched the lead horses to the front of the wagon.

"Stop yer day dreamin' and get up on the wagon."

Rosa was sitting up on the front of the wagon with her mother and her father was riding behind them leading the horses that he was taking to sell. The early morning sun was shining and the birds were singing as they travelled along. Four other families were travelling behind them and they all made a pretty parade, each wagon gleaming clean and painted in bright colours.

"Are ye gonnae be telling fortunes Mam?"

"If Ah'm asked."

"Can ye tell mine?"

Mary laughed, "Ah dinnae need tae be a fortune teller tae see what's comin' for ye, it's a' Eddie, Eddie, Eddie."

"But will we have bairns Ma?"

"Aye, lass ye'll have bairns, of course ye'll have bairns."

"Have ye looked then?"

"Naw, Ah've no' looked an' Ah'm no' gonnae look."

"Why no' Ma?"

"It'll be a nice surprise when it comes."

That answer pleased Rosa, but the truth of the matter was that Mary was afraid to look. One of the curses of being able to see the future is that sometimes you see things that you cannot change and after seeing these things, you know that you can do nothing but worry about them.

Musselburgh was seven miles from Edinburgh, and they would water and exercise their horses at the banks of the River Esk. They were all looking forward to getting to the fair for they knew that the showmen would be there with their galloping horses' carousel, which had only been around for a few years. It was such a novelty that it attracted hundreds of fairgoers and they would be camped quite near the fairground. Even knowing that it would be busy at Musselburgh, it didn't take away from their surprise and delight at the crowds that were milling about as they drove over the cobbled stones of the High Street and past Merkat Cross.

There were other families behind and ahead of them and their procession drew gasps from pedestrians going about their business. Finally, they arrived and queued to enter the field where they would camp for the next few days. Other travellers were already setting up stalls to display and sell their wares. Some would come and lend a hand with unpacking, and to share the latest news. The Wilson's, the Boswell's, and the Stewarts called hello and gave a cheery wave.

Chapter 38

The energy around the field was electric and Rosa was bouncing with excitement. Mary tried to calm her but it was hopeless.

"Mind yer ane business Rosa and dinnae let yer Da catch you lookin' at the lads," her mother whispered.

"I'm no' lookin at the lads Mam, Ah was jist lookin' for…" her face burning with embarrassment.

"I know who yer lookin for, it's that Eddie McGuigan. A guid boy mind ye, but dinnae show yer keen."

"I like him Ma, he asked me to remember him last year."

"Wheesht, here's yer Da!"

Suddenly she caught sight of him and her heart skipped a beat as her cheeks began to glow bright red.

"Ma," she whispered.

"I see him."

Rosa kept her eyes downcast as Eddie approached, and not once did Eddie look in her direction.

"Excuse me, Aunty Mary," he said, as was the custom in his culture, "Could Ah speak tae Uncle John?"

"Ye've never had a problem speakin' tae him before Eddie, dae ye think ye might have wan the noo."

Mary laughed to herself as she watched this boy, now a young man, she had loved since he was a baby. Eddie was mortified but he knew that his Auntie Mary was teasing him.

John's heart almost stopped as he came around the wagon and saw Eddie there because he had a notion that he knew what was coming and he would never be ready for this. He glowered at him, "Eddie."

"Uncle John, a word."

"Well, spit it out and Ah'm warnin' ye, Ah'm nae in the best o moods."

Eddie was not happy at John's sharp tone and was equally sharp with his reply. "Ah could come back an' see ye."

"Jist git on wi' it lad. Ah've things tae dae."

Eddie was a confident lad, but what he was about to say meant so much to him that he wanted to create the best impression, nevertheless he was not prepared to be intimidated. He took a deep breath, straightened his shoulders, looked his uncle in the eye, and said, "It's an important thing Ah wish tae speak tae ye about, but if ye huvnae time tae be civil Ah'll come back."

Realising that he had been a bit harsh with Eddie, John tried to start again.

"Jist haud yer horses' lad, ye got me on the wrong foot. Ah feel Ah know whit ye want to speak tae me about an it's churnin' in ma' stomach. Say yer piece."

As John stepped closer he moved to put his arm over Eddies shoulder and realised with some shock that the lad was no longer a lad in fact he was taller and broader than John. He shrugged, embarrassed by the realisation, and stuck his hands in his pocket.

"Let's take a walk Eddie."

Eddie was the next to speak, he stopped mid stride and turned to look John in the eye. He took a deep breath, and said, "Ah've loved yer lass since Ah was wee, an' she was just a babe. Ah've watched her grow and become the beautiful lass like the flower ye named her for. The past four years Ah've worked and saved and every penny is for Rosa's future."

John knew it was coming but now that it had, his heart was pounding in his chest as he looked at the man who would take his daughter away from him. He couldn't find the breath to speak, and he and Eddie stared at each other for what felt to both of them like an eternity.

"Ah'm askin' ye for her hand man," he almost shouted.

Finally, John spoke "Same time, same place, next year, if ye still feel the same ye can ask her yirsel, an' if she agrees ye can marry on the first day of May at the Tinkers Heart."

Eddie did a dance right there in front of John.

"She'll say aye, I know it."

As John walked back to his wagon he could see Rosa helping her mother and his heart swelled with pride and some sadness because he knew that in the not too distant future she would be away with Eddie looking after her on family.

"Ah've jist seen that young Eddie," he said to no one in particular, but really so that Rosa could hear. "Turned into a fine man," he said, as he climbed into his wagon. He poured himself a whisky and sat there and that's where Mary found him, sitting staring straight ahead, his face wet with tears. She sat beside him, placed her hand in his, and gave it a comforting squeeze. She felt as he did, proud and happy for her daughter, but desperately sad at the thought of her leaving them.

Rosa had finished helping her mother and she changed from her travelling clothes to her new dress that she and her mother had patiently sewn together. The skirt was bright red with gold and green abstract patterns and the bodice had a red trimmed white insert with black lacing down the centre. She wandered across to the river and sat quietly by herself admiring the activity around her and looking at her skirt from time to time delighted with the bright blues and reds of the fabric. She was waiting for Eddie and she knew that he would find her. She wondered what he had said to her father, and more she wondered what he had said to him. She had butterflies in her stomach as she thought of the conversation that they might have had. She kept glancing up to see if she could see him, but she remembered what her mother had said about not looking as though she was too eager. How could she not be too eager, she loved him with all her being, he was the other part of her, and then he was there, right beside her.

"Oh Eddie, "Ah'm pleased tae see ye."

As he sat on the grass beside her he gave her a red rose and said, "Ah'm fair pleased tae see ye tae. Ah spoke tae yer Da," he said, grinning from ear to ear, holding her hand and looking into her eyes. "Whit did he say Eddie?"

"He said Aye, no' like that though, his exact words were 'Same time same place next year an' if ye feel the same ye can merry on the first o' May at the Tinkers Heart. Whit dae ye make o' that Rosa?"

Rosa's hands flew to her mouth, "Are ye kiddin' me? Did he really say that? We can be wed at The Tinkers Heart! Oh, my that'll be grand. Ah'm fair excited Eddie."

"Jist a year and a bit, on the first of May we'll marry above Loch Fyne at the Tinkers Heart, and Ah promise Ah'll love ye forever Rosa if ye'll have me."

He took a beautiful gold ring from his waistcoat pocket and placed it on her finger. She gazed at the tiny diamonds in the shape of a flower and said, "Aye Eddie, Ah will marry ye," as he kissed the happy tears on her face.

They spent a while sitting there on the grass expressing their love for each other in words to each other and in their eyes. They had no thought of anyone else but themselves. Eventually they had to make their way back to Rosa's wagon where Mary and John were waiting for their return. All eyes were on them as they made their way across the field for news travels like wild fire and everyone knew now that Rosa and Eddie were betrothed. Mary and John were sitting outside their wagon as they approached and Rosa ran to her mother holding out her left hand to show off her ring. "Look Mam, look at what Eddie has given me! It's beautiful."

Mary and John stood and each in turn they embraced both Eddie and Rosa.

"It's lovely Rosa, Ah'm happy for ye."

That night everyone gathered to share in the good news; they sang and danced, they played fiddles and accordions, and they generally overindulged until the early hours of the morning. There was another surprise that night and that was the arrival of Eddie's cousin Tam, who was in his early thirties. He had been off travelling; some said he was hoping to find a wife, others laughed and said he was trying to avoid getting married, but Tam had no such thoughts, he was a wanderer but he had reached the point where he was ready to go back to his roots. Tams arrival made it a double celebration.

"Where have ye been Tam," John asked.

"Och man, Ah've been all over Scotland, away as far as Inverness an' beyond." Someone laughed and joked, "Aye yer feet must be loupin' Tam. Everyone laughed at the joke and then he was asked "Whit have ye done?"

"Ah've done a bit o' everythin', worked wi' sheep for a while, worked wi' some Highland Cattle tae, an' horses, but the best was when Ah was workin' wi' a builder, makin doors an' the like."

Eddie came over, offered him a bottle of beer, and sat down beside him. "Ah'm right glad yer back Tam. Will ye bide a while?"

"Aye that's me, Ah'm ready tae settle."

"Can Ah ask ye a favour then?"

Tam turned and looked at him, "Aye Eddie, whit's up?"

"Will ye stand wi' me at ma weddin Tam?" Tam stood up and as he did so did Eddie. Eddie wondered what Tam was thinking because he just stood there looking at him, and then he said, "That's no' a favour Eddie, that's an honour, It would be my pleasure tae stand wi' ye," and he threw his arms around Eddie and gave his younger cousin a crushing hug. The two men stood laughing at each other. "Ye nearly broke ma ribs Tam," said Eddie

"Ye fair took ma breath away," replied Tam both of them laughing at their own enthusiasm. It was a night to remember and everyone enjoyed the festivities.

Chapter 39

The following day everyone had their stalls or tables set up and the crowds were pouring in. Some folk were there to ride on the carousel horses or visit the side stalls where they could throw hoops at pegs pinned to a wall, or throw wooden balls at a rows of coconuts balanced precariously on posts. Some would be lucky enough to win a balloon or better still a goldfish. Mary had a fancy tent, made of four tall poles stuck into the ground covered on three sides with fancy purple fabric. Another length of ornate red and gold silk cloth draped across the front to allow eager customers a hint of privacy. A board with a hand painted image of a large crystal ball stood outside the tent. Mary wore a colourful silk wrap over her normal clothes and fashioned a red silk scarf over her hair. Large gold hoops in her ears and several thin gold bangles on her wrists created the image she was trying to portray. This made no difference to what she would say, but it was expected. Inside the tent were two chairs with a table set between them. The table was covered with a purple silk cloth and on the table was an elaborate candleholder with a thick white candle burning brightly, Mary's scrying glass, and a deck of ordinary playing cards. Mary only used the playing cards occasionally for they were only useful to her for looking at what was happening, but she could never see in them why these things would occur.

Within the hour, there were queues of women eagerly waiting to hear what Mary had to say. When a customer come in Mary would tell them to sit in the chair opposite her and place their hands on the table with their palms upwards. First, she would sit quietly looking at their hands as though she was palm reading; in truth that was not Mary's skill, but it gave the customer a moment to settle and then Mary would place her hands on top of the customers. After a few moments, Mary would close her eyes and allow sensations and vibrations the freedom to flow from the customers psyche to hers. This was how Mary could predict things with such accuracy. When she was ready, Mary would open her eyes and look directly into her customers eyes. Some found this captivating, others disconcerting, but Mary, always accurate, would begin to tell them things about themselves. Sometimes she was so accurate in describing events that had already happened that she scared her customer. Other customers wanted to know more, and Mary would tell them to choose some cards. If they were willing to pay extra, Mary would uncover her scrying glass and begin to gaze into it until images appeared.

She had been working steadily for a few hours when a woman came in and sat down as she was bid, but as soon as she was seated, she said, "I don't want my fortune told."

"Why have ye come then?"

"I have something that I hope you will take from me, because I don't know what else to do." The woman opened her bag and drew out a small package wrapped in black satin and passed it across the table to Mary.

"Whit's in it?"

"Tarot cards," replied the woman.

Goosebumps stood on Mary's back and neck. She had heard of Tarot cards, but had never yet seen them. She looked at the package eager to open it and at the same time fearful. She drew them towards her and carefully opened the package. Inside was a cardboard box, worn at the edges with a well-used look about them Mary asked, "Where did ye get these?"

"We just moved into a new house and I found them when I was cleaning out old boxes that were left in the loft. I opened them and had a look."

"Why are ye givin' them tae me?"

"I thought you would know what to do with them."

"Why are ye no' keepin' them for yer self."

The woman began to cry, "They frightened me, and I am too scared to throw them away in case I get bad luck."

"Dinnae be daft. Ah'll take them an Ah'll tell ye yer future for free."

"No! No, thank you very much, I don't want a reading, I just want to be rid of them," and at that she jumped up and left the tent.

Mary shrugged and thought to herself that if the woman didn't want them, she was glad to have them. She was too busy to do anything more than put them in her bag as there was a queue of people waiting to see her. Word of Mary's accuracy at the fair soon spread and for the next few days, she hardly had time to lift her head. By nine o'clock each evening, Mary was more than ready to close her curtain over and bring in her board. She would go into her wagon and lie down, exhausted from seeing so many people.

Rosa looked after her mother during the day making sure that she stopped for a drink of tea or something to eat. On the last day, when everyone was finished, all the Gypsies would dismantle rides, pack away their stalls, and then gather in the middle of the field and have a farewell party. The next morning, they would be up and away at the break of dawn and by the time local people were moving about, going to work or going shopping, there would be no sign of them. The journey home was a quiet one, as most of them were too tired to think never mind chatter, but overall the fair had been a great success. John's thoughts were on horses, for he had sold everything that he had taken with him and he knew that he would have to build his sale stock up for other fairs. Mary's mind was on Rosa, and that this was probably be one of the last fairs that they would go to together, and Rosa, all she could think of was Eddie. She kept glancing to the ring on her finger, admiring it, smiling to herself and thinking of Eddie.

Chapter 40

In the days, weeks, and months that followed all Rosa could talk about or think about was her wedding. She was impatient and wished that it could be this coming May that they would be married, but she would abide by her father's wishes and wait until after the next fair at Musselburgh. Often she would sit and talk with her cousin Lizzie whom she had asked to be her maid of honour and they would giggle as they chatted. Mary would see them and her heart would swell with pride as she watched her beautiful daughter.

They went to local fairs until the end of the summer and then they occupied their time with preparing things to sell around doors for Christmas time. The women and girls were always making something that they could later sell. Rosa spent much of her time gathering and making things for her bottom drawer. From the time they were little, girls got into the habit of putting things into a trunk that they would keep until they got married themselves. This was common practise in Scotland and everyone did it, not just Gypsies. On cold winter nights, Rosa and her mother would often open the trunk and look through her things. She had white linen pillowcases and sheets that she had patiently sat pulling ten weft threads an inch below the hems, and then gathering the warp threads together using coloured embroidery silks, making patterns of little crosses. There would be gifts given to her on her wedding day from guests who would travel from everywhere to witness her marriage to Eddie. Eddie was busy too, he was building a fine wagon for them to start their married life, and Rosa would not know anything about it until she was his wife.

There was nothing else for it except to endure the long cold winter and look forward to the summer months when they could once more meet again at Musselburgh or other fairs that they both might be attending. Everyone kept busy but being apart was difficult for the young lovers.

At the first sign of spring, Mary began to look out boxes of things that she had stored away that she would need for the coming fairs. She sat outside her wagon and pulled out her fancy fabrics that she used to create her fortune-telling tent. She shook them out and draped them over the wheels of the wagon to air. When she looked in the bag where her candleholder and accoutrements were stored, she came across the black satin wrap. At first, she couldn't think what it was and then suddenly she remembered the woman who had given it to her at the Musselburgh Fair. She took the wrap into the wagon, sat at her table, and carefully opened the satin parcel. Inside was the cardboard box of Tarot cards. The edges of the dark blue box were scuffed and worn and she tentatively opened the flap at one end and drew out the cards. The first card that she saw had a picture of a vagabond wearing a colourful tunic and carrying his possessions wrapped in cloth, tied to a stick, and jauntily balanced over his shoulder. The sun was shining above his head and he was standing at what looked like the edge of a cliff. In the background, she could see the sea. She did her best to try to read the words written below his feet. Strictly speaking, many Gypsies couldn't read or write, but they often had a little knowledge that would enable them to figure out what was written. She knew the first word was 'The' and then she laughed to herself as she realised that the second was 'Fool', she felt like a fool as she laughed.

Her heart was pounding in her chest as she spread the cards out in front of her and then she realised that this was going to be very difficult for her to understand. She counted them first, there were seventy-eight cards in all, and they all had pictures. She sat and thought for a bit and then she began to put similar cards together. There were ten cards with Cups, ten with Branches, which in fact we know as Wands, ten with Coins, we know as Pentacles, and ten with Swords. She couldn't understand the roman numerals, but by counting the Cups, Branches, Coins, and Swords, she was able to discern that they related to each number. Mary placed each individual pile in a row and then began to look at the remaining cards. There were four Kings, four Queens, four pages and four Knights, each of them had Cups, Branches, Coins, and Swords, so she added these to the appropriate piles. She counted the remaining cards, there were twenty-two. She put them to one side and looked at the ones she had put into order.

She sat there looking and thinking trying to figure out what she was missing because she was sure that she was missing something obvious. She went to the chitty prop and poured herself a cup of tea.

"Dae ye need me Mam?" questioned Rosa who was sitting chatting at the fire.

"Naw Hinny, jist bide where ye are."

She went back into her wagon and sat once more at the table looking at the piles of cards and then she jumped up, fetched her bag, and took out the playing cards. She separated them into their suits; there were thirteen cards in all, King, Queen, Jack, in the hearts, diamonds, clubs, and spades. She was tingling now. She counted the playing cards, there were fifty-two. She compared them, the two lots of cards and then she laid each of them in a row. The top row had all the Branches then the Cups, then the Coins and finally the Swords. On the next row below the Cups, she placed the hearts, and then below the diamonds she placed the Coins. That left two suits to figure out. She now had Branches and Swords to place, *"That must mean that spades or clubs are branches or swords.*" She decided that clubs should be with Swords and spades should be with Branches. She counted each pile again only to find after several counts that the Tarot cards had an extra card in each suit and then the penny dropped and she knew what was different. She took out the four knights from each of the Tarot cards and counted again and this time they matched. She muttered to herself trying to understand the puzzle,

"So the plain cards have fifty two. The Tarot cards have fifty two, plus four knights, plus twenty two others?"

This was an awakening for Mary and she almost didn't know what to do with herself as she realised that ordinary playing cards actually came from Tarot cards. She had so much to think about, she gathered all the playing cards together and put them away. Then she gathered the Tarot cards that she had been working with and put them in a pile to one side. It was time to apply herself to the mystery of the twenty-two remaining cards, but the effort had left her feeling spent and she decided that she would study the remaining cards in a day or two.

For the next few days, Mary went about her normal routine, however, her mind was busy trying to work out what she had discovered about the Tarot cards, and she was eager to find a minute so that she could sit quietly and study the twenty-two cards that were still a mystery to her.

Chapter 41

For the next few months, life continued as normal but at every opportunity, Mary took herself off to sit quietly and study her Tarot cards. She had managed to decipher the Roman Numerals on the major cards by comparing the numbers on the suit cards, that helped her to put the major cards into their sequence, and each day she laid the majors out in a row and tried to understand them. Finally, it all clicked into place for her, and she realised that the major cards were the cause of changes and the minor cards were predictable reactions, good, or otherwise. The Cups were all brightly coloured and told her about love. In contrast, the Swords were darker in colour and appeared to show problems. It was as she was looking at these things, that she realised the significance of them all. Wands were for springtime, ideas thoughts, and growth. Cups were summer cards and told her about love and romance. The Coins made her think about earning money and she concluded that this must mean harvest and autumn. If that was the case then the Swords were winter. Swords were weapons, but they could also be tools, consequently, they were about action. Each suit had its fair share of good and bad cards that would help her in her predictions.

John made her a new board showing images of the tarot cards to display outside her tent at the Musselburgh fair. It was only later, when she was using the tarot cards for customer readings that she realised that every time she shuffled the cards, if one fell out, it was conveying a message for the person that she was reading for, because the same card would appear during the reading. She was never tempted to read them for herself, in fact she was a little afraid of them, but she would never have admitted that to anyone. She also realised that the images depicted in the cards were personifications of the customer and how that customer felt or would feel.

Mary became so adept at reading the Tarot cards that she could now tell people what things would happen, why these things would happen and how best to act or react. If someone had a problem, Mary could tell that person how to avoid it. If avoiding it was not possible, Mary could at least tell them how long it would be before the issue was resolved and what would happen next. When there were opportunities, Mary could tell her customers about them so that they were able to take full advantage of them. She could predict the timing of things with an accuracy that sometimes even surprised her.

It was common for there to be more than one fortuneteller at fairs, but they only read ordinary playing cards which Mary now knew only told part of the story. Mary now understood the difference, and because of this insight, her reputation grew even more and she always had the biggest queue. As customers came and went from Mary's tent, Rosa stood nearby in case Mary needed anything. At the end of the day, when Mary spoke to her mother, she was laughing.

"Ma, ye should hear whit folk are saying when they come oot yer tent."

"Whit did ye hear?"

"Well there was a woman in the queue waiting for her mither who was in wi' ye an' when the mither came oot she slapped her daughter an' said *'Ye should a' told me ye were havin' a bairn instead o' lettin' me hear it fae a fortune teller.'* Rosa and her mother laughed at this, and Mary was delighted that the cards were proving to be so accurate.

Later that evening, Rosa and Eddie sat with the others enjoying the time that they had together. Eddie, handsome as ever, was wearing his red neckerchief and he had given a matching one to Rosa that she was wearing in her hair. This was a sign to anyone who didn't know them that they were betrothed to each other. They talked about their forthcoming wedding at The Tinkers Heart.

"Whit happens after the weddin' Eddie?"

"Ah'll kiss ye till ye think ye cannae breathe," he replied laughing.

Rosa thumped him playfully on his shoulder, "Ah dinnae mean that, Ah mean where will we go? Where will we live?"

"Well Ah' would like tae bide at the Green, but Ah'd like tae go other places tae."

"Wi' can dae a' that Rosa, wi' can spend a couple o' months jist here and there, visitin' friends an' kin an' then come back an' settle on the Green if ye like."

"Aye Ah'd like that fine."

"Will wi' have bairns Eddie?"

"As many as ye like."

They made a pretty picture, both of them sitting holding hands and with eye for no one but each other. Rosa was crying when it was time to leave and Eddie had to be strong for both of them.

"It'll no' be that long Rosa, ye'll see, the winter will fly past an' afore ye ken ye'll be climbin' the hill tae the Tinkers Heart an Ah'll be there afore ye."

He took her by the hand and walked her back to her wagon where her mother and father were packing up. Mary had dismantled her tent and put her candleholder and scrying glass into her bag. She wrapped the Tarot cards in the original piece of satin and put them in the bag too. She wouldn't need any of these things until the next fair. They all said their farewells and Eddie stood and watched as Rosa, John, and Mary left the fair. He was as sad as Rosa was, but he knew that the next time he would see her he would never have to leave her again. For the next few months, he would concentrate on getting the new wagon ready for her, and he would put all his energy and love into that. Now that Tam was back, he would enjoy sharing the work with him.

Rosa climbed into the back of the wagon, lay down on the bench, and cried. John and Mary knew that she was crying and John whispered to Mary, "Are ye gonnae go back an' see tae her?"

Mary looked at John and said, "Dae ye think that Ah can say onythin' that will ease her hurt John?"

"Naw, Ah suppose yer right enough, better tae let her cry."

The wagon trundled along and eventually Rosa fell into a sleep. When they arrived back at the camp, they began to store away things that they only used for fairs. While they carried out their task, Rosa spoke quietly to her mother.

"Ah had a funny dream when Ah was sleepin' on the way back Ma."

Mary looked at her, "Whit aboot?"

"Me an' Eddie an' a bairn."

"Was that no' a guid dream?"

"Ah'm no' sure Ma, ye see Ah was standin' at the edge o' a field, an' Eddie was at the other end o' it. Ah could see him clear enough, but he had the bairn in his arms an' he was walking away an' wavin' tae me."

The hackles stood on Mary's back and she felt as though the colour was draining from her face. She turned her head so that Rosa wouldn't see her reaction while she pretended that it was of no importance. "Och it's probably jist yer mind playing tricks on ye. Sure ye had jist said cheerio tae Eddie an' yer thinking aboot yer weddin an' startin' a family, dinnae worry yer self. It was jist a dream."

Mary was worried, no Mary was more than worried, she was sick to her stomach. and had to take herself off to the dunny so that she could cover her face with her hands and weep. She was not sure what the dream meant, but she was afraid of the worst thing that could happen and she didn't want her fears to be seen by anyone, especially not John or Rosa.

Chapter 42

Mary watched Rosa carefully over the coming months, making sure that she didn't do anything that would bring harm to her, but as time passed, she began to relax and believe what she had told Rosa at the time, *"It was jist a bad dream."* Gradually the memory of the dream began to disappear, and all they thought, and talked about was the coming wedding, but Mary had a niggling feeling that she couldn't quite understand.

"Look Mam, look whit Ah've got in ma trunk," called Rosa

Mary sat beside her and together they looked at all the fine things that Rosa and some of the families had made for her. Mary asked her, "Are ye worried aboot onythin' Rosa?"

"Naw Ma, should Ah be?"

Mary laughed, "Naw Rosa, but have ye spoke aboot where ye will go after yer wed?"

"Oh that, aye, wi' will go travellin' for a bit, see some different places and visit folks we've no' seen for a while. There are some o' Eddie's family that Ah don't ken yet. Ah think he wants tae show me aff," she replied laughing, "but dinnae worry we're comin' back here tae settle on the Green." Then she said, "Ah'm wonderin' whit dress tae wear though."

Mary smiled and went to another trunk that was for her special things. She unpacked it carefully and then produced a brown cardboard box tied with string from the bottom of the trunk. "See whit ye think o' this then," she said as she handed it to Rosa. Rosa took the parcel and reverently untied the piece of string and opened the box. There were two brown paper packages inside; she lifted out the first one and carefully unfolded the paper and she caught a glimpse of pale blue cloth, with tiny sprigs of white daisies all over it. She lifted it out and realised that it was a dress made of fine cotton lawn. She held it up in front of her and looked down at it. A faded blue ribbon inserted through the scooped neckline, trimmed with handmade lace in the same fashion as the long sleeves. There was a white lace pinafore, which came to a point at the front. Mary had tears in her eyes as she helped Rosa to put the dress on.

"Ah wore this when Ah wed yer Da an' ma' Mam wore it when she got wed tae. Dae ye like it Rosa?"

"Oh Ma, Ah love it, can Ah really wear it?"

"Aye hinny it would make me proud tae see ye in it."

"Whit's in the other parcel?"

Mary opened the second parcel, and took out a long net veil, trimmed all around in the same lace as the dress. She placed the veil on Rosa's head and then lifted a circlet of tiny handmade flowers and placed that on top to hold the veil in place.

"Ye look bonny Rosa, quick now tak it aff afore yer Da comes back, and Ah'll get it a' ready for yur big day."

The worst of the winter was past and everyone was looking forward to Rosa's wedding. There were daffodils everywhere and it was almost as though Mother Nature was celebrating too. All Mary could think about was Rosa leaving with Eddie. She was going to miss her terribly and although she tried to be brave, she was anxious about how long she would be away travelling.

The wedding date was fast approaching when Rosa asked Mary if she had ever been to The Tinkers Heart.

"Aye Ah have, its lovely there."

"How far is it Mam?"

"Ah think aboot four days travel?"

"That sounds a long way Ma, Ah don't ken where that is."

"Well when wi' leave here wi'll head for Old Kilpatrick and camp up there for the night and then the next day wi' head for Helensburgh, ye'll like it there. From Helensburgh wi' go tae Arrochar. That's the last stop afore wi' head ower Hells Glen tae the Tinkers Heart. Wait till ye see it, fae the top o' the hill ye can see across the water tae the castle on the other side o' the loch. It's a big occasion, folks will come fae everywhere tae go tae a weddin' at The Tinkers Heart. There'll even be folk there that wi' dinnae ken."

"Why is it called the Tinkers Heart?"

"Some say it was a place tae honour Gypsy lads that died in a war, a rebellion a long time ago, an' then oor kind, knowin' it was a special place sometimes got wed there, some blessed their new bairns there, and some went there tae pay their respects tae their loved ones that had passed. Its aye extra special when a couple weds at The Tinkers Heart.

"Ah didnae ken it was so special Mam."

"Well yer Da thinks ye are special an' he aye wants nothin' but the best for his Rosa. It' just a wee heart shape lined wi' quartz stones that sparkle in the sunlight, but it's got a special feelin' tae it."

Later, when her father arrived back, Rosa ran to him and threw her arms around his neck.

"Whit's up wi' ye lass?"

"Nothin Da, Ah jist want ye tae know that Ah love ye and Ah'm gonnae miss ye when Ah'm away."

When Rosa let go and ran off to join her cousin, no doubt to talk of what she had learned, John stood there with tears in his eyes and his heart full of love. When he saw Mary, he asked her, "Whit was that a' aboot, did ye see her. She nearly knocked me on ma backside when she jumped into ma arms, did ye see her?"

Mary was laughing when she replied, "Aye a' saw her, she was askin' aboot The Tinkers Heart. She's excited John."

Chapter 43

Mary was crying, she could see Rosa lying flat out and there was something wrong with Rosa. Her lips were moving, but Mary couldn't hear what she was saying. Over and over, she shouted, "Whit's wrang Rosa, Ah cannae hear ye, whit's wrang?" Eddie was there too, and he looked petrified. Rosa reached out for Eddie but she was getting further away from them and Mary began to scream, but no noise came out of her mouth. She could hear her own heart beating in her chest and she could feel someone grabbing her by the shoulders, trying to pull her away, but she just wanted to get to Rosa so she fought with all her might.

"Mary! Mary!" John was shaking her and eventually she came out of her nightmare, but she still felt as though she was in it. John was alarmed and Rosa, wakened by her mother's distress, was frantically asking, "Ma, Ma whits the matter?"

"Go an' see if the water is still hot in the big kettle an' make yer Ma some tea, if no' jist bring her water." Rosa hurried off to the chitty prop and John turned to Mary.

"Whit's up Mary, whit's up?"

"Ah had a really bad dream John."

"Dae ye want tae tell me whit it wis?"

"Ah cannae remember." Mary was lying and John knew that she didn't want to talk about it so he didn't push her. He took the cup from Rosa and gave it to Mary to drink. "Dae ye think ye can sleep or dae ye want tae take a walk?" Mary was surprised that John would ask her this, she guessed that he knew she wouldn't speak of it and perhaps he thought she would speak of it outside.

"Try an' get some sleep Rosa, Ah'll just take a walk wi' yer Ma."

Rosa got back under her blankets and John and Mary threw a blanket over their shoulders and left the wagon. They walked across the field and through the trees. All was still, but for a few snorts from the horses, wondering what was going on. When they reached the river, they sat down.

"Dae ye want tae tell me whit was in yer dream?"

Mary was quiet and John was patient.

"Tell me Mary."

"Ah cannae put it into words in case Ah make it happen."

"Wis it aboot Rosa?"

Mary nodded and began to cry again.

"Ye ken Mary, ye have been anxious aboot Rosa leavin' would that no' make ye have bad dreams?"

Still crying silently, Mary nodded once more. John sat there with his arms about her; he didn't know what else to do. After a while, the both went back to the wagon and crept in quietly to avoid disturbing Rosa, but she was still awake, worried about her mother.

"Are ye better Mam?"

"Aye go back tae sleep hinny it was just a bad dream, Ah cannae even remember whit it wis aboot noo."

Relieved, Rosa settled down and was soon asleep again.

It was the dream that prompted Mary to do something that she promised herself that she wouldn't. She decided to look at the Tarot cards, but she didn't want anyone to see her. She was rummaging about in one of her boxes under the wagon when John asked her what she was looking for.

"Ah'm jist looking for ma stuff for the next fair," she said.

"Dae ye need a hand?"

"Naw John, Ah've found ma stuff. She made as if she was just airing her cloths but what she really wanted was her little bag that had her fortune telling things. She opened it up at took out the black satin wrapped Tarot cards and then she wrapped her fancy silk cloth around them and called, "Ah'm just away tae the river tae gie this silk a rinse in fresh water John."

She headed off through the trees to the river and sat on the grass. She sat there for a while with the wrapped cards between her hands, pondering on questions that she could ask, but in the end she decided that she would just let the cards speak to her. She closed her eyes, steadied her breathing, and opened the satin wrap. She took out the cardboard box, flipped open the end and took out the cards. She shuffled them in her hands mixing them thoroughly trying to keep her mind free from any thoughts, and then she fanned the cards face down in front of her. For the first time since she had been given the cards, she wished that she knew someone whom she could talk to about Tarot cards because now that she was doing it for herself, she was afraid of doing something wrong and misreading them. She passed her right hand over the cards, about two inches above them, trying to sense which one she should choose first. She drew one card towards her and apprehensively turned it over. It was the High Priestess. That was one card that she didn't fully understand and couldn't interpret its meaning. She wasn't aware that the High Priestess represented hidden information, things that she was not yet meant to know about. Because she didn't understand its meaning, seeing this card did not worry her. She had no concept that this card could bring good or bad so she had no reason to fear it. The next card that she drew was the one with two Cups and she smiled happily when she saw this because it was two young lovers exchanging promises. It was plainly depicting Rosa and Eddie's wedding day. The third that she drew was a major card, the one with the wheel on it. This card made her feel content because the illustration was a large wagon wheel. *'That'll be the journey goin' tae or leavin' the weddin'.'* She drew a third card toward herself and turned it over to reveal the card with ten Coins. The illustration was of lots of people, children and adults, *'That must be the weddin' party,'* she thought to herself, and gathering the cards together, wrapped them in the satin and gave her silk cloth a quick rinse in the river, just in case John noticed. When she went back, she draped her silk cloth over the wheel to let it dry. She was much happier now and content to believe that she had only had the dream because she was worrying about missing Rosa.

Chapter 44

Over the next few weeks, leading up to the wedding, Mary was more content and happy, and they were all looking forward to travelling to The Tinkers Heart. The whole camp could talk of nothing else, but Rosa and Eddie's forthcoming wedding. Those women that could sew were making pretty skirts, tops, or dresses, or cutting cloth into squares to fasten their hair. Those who couldn't sew well were bothering others to help them. The men as usual took all this frantic activity in their stride and left the women to steam their better clothes over boiling kettles. They would wear a waistcoat with a white shirt and colourful neckerchief, but it was women's work to organise that. They paid heed to the horses and the wagons making sure that the wheels were in good condition to make the journey without mishap. Two men would stay behind and miss the wedding celebrations. They would look after the horses or anything else during the time everyone was away. Some made plans to collect provisions or things that they could re-sell at fairs on the return journey. All was well, for a little while anyway, and then just days before they were about to leave, Mary had the dream again. This time John was quick to react and woke Mary before Rosa was disturbed.

"Will ye tell me the dream Mary?"

Mary didn't want to share the dream with John because it would worry him sick. There was no point in them both being worried, and she didn't want to put it into words.

"Ah cannae remember it John."

John knew he was wasting his time trying to force Mary to share the dream if she didn't want to, so he just sat comforting her. It was the best that he could do. The following days were difficult for Mary. She was unsettled and afraid to close her eyes at night in case the dream returned. She was pale and had dark circles round her eyes. She had lost her appetite and even Rosa was beginning to notice that all was not well with her mother.

"Ah'm worried aboot ma Mam," she said to her father.

"Dinnae be, she's fine, she's jist no' sleepin' well, she'll miss ye when yer away, but it'll no' be that long till yer back again and a' this grief will jist be a memory. Ye'll see, after the weddin she'll be fine, jist let her be."

Finally, the day arrived when they were ready to set off. As always, they started their journey at first light. Mary was anxious but she was excited too and she was hopeful that now the journey was beginning she would be too tired to dream. They stopped as planned at some spare ground in Old Kilpatrick and camped there for the night. There was a good campfire burning brightly, boxes out to sit around it, and that was all the reason they needed to sing songs and drink a few beers. The next day, another early rise, and they were on their way. Their journey took them along the River Clyde past Dumbarton Castle, through Cardross and then to Helensburgh. They were beginning to see other travellers in the distance and Rosa wondered if Eddie was among them. That night they camped and partied and everyone was enjoying the excursion.

By the time they reached Arrochar the following day, Rosa's excitement was bubbling over. Mary however was still a bit unsettled. Rosa was sitting up in front with her father and Mary was sitting inside, the rolling of the wagon making her sleepy. Before she lay down, she took the opportunity to draw one Tarot card. It was the one with six Cups. She sat quietly looking at the illustration. There were two people in it; one looked older, possibly a child, the other could be an older child or an adult because the second was stooped over presenting the smaller one with flowers. She realised that it looked like a reunion. She felt relieved that it was a good card for she knew that going to a wedding she was bound to meet people from her past. She was glad that the card did not show something that she should worry about.

Finally, they arrived amid the great gathering of Gypsies camping at the bottom of the hill, and more arriving all the time, but there was a surprise in store for Mary, one that she hadn't seen coming. All her instincts were on Rosa's wedding and the dreams that she had been having, but this surprise would bring her great joy. People were moving about saying hello to folks they hadn't seen for a while, others were sitting around the fire and at the edge of the crowd Mary saw a woman staring at her and smiling. At first, all she saw was a familiar face, and she smiled nodded then looked away trying to place who she was, and then in a moment of realisation, her heart almost stopped when she recognised the face. "Johnny! Johnny!" she called using his name as she had when they were young. She was crying tears of joy as she started to run, she could hardly get the words out, "Its ma sister, its ma sister."

Coralina and Mary ran to each other both crying, both hugging, and then drawing back to look into each other's faces. It was a touching sight to see. John was grinning from ear to ear, and had to wait his turn to embrace his sister-in-law. It was a few moments before Mary and John realised that there were others standing close by. Robert stood off to one side waiting and then it was just a melee as Coralina introduced her family; her grown up daughter Emily, with her husband Edward and their young son Paul.

"Oh! ma sisters a granny!" laughed Mary as she swept young Paul into her arms smothering him with kisses. John and Robert shook hands and embraced warmly.

"How are ye Johnny?"

"Aye it's a while since Ah was called Johnny, she only says Johnny when she's emotional," he laughed, nodding at Mary.

Mary embraced her niece Emily, and introduced Rosa to her Aunt Coralina, her Uncle Robert, and her little cousin Paul. For the next few hours, they shared what each had been doing.

"Ah never thought this day would come Coralina, ma heart is jist burstin' wi' happiness. How far have ye come, how did ye ken?"

"We've had the rent o' a farm near Oban for the last ten years. Paul's family are mindin' it for us while we're here. This was too guid a chance tae miss." The two sisters, grown women now, sat together holding hands, and reminiscing. "Robert was worried that he wouldnae be welcome, but Ah told him time heals. Ah hope Rosa and her fella come by the farm when they are on their travels for they will be welcome an' we're anxious tae get tae know them better."

Her Aunt Coralina fascinated Rosa, and she thought about the stories she had heard of her running away with the miller's son. She didn't have to think long about whether or not she would have done the same for Eddie because she knew that if they were separated she would run to him in a heartbeat. She found the opportunity to talk to her cousin Emily about it later. "Aye, Ah know the story well, Ma an' Da have talked about it afore. It's really romantic, but it must have been hard for them tae, leaving family an' the like. Whit aboot yer fella, Ah hear his name's Eddie?"

"Aye, an' Ah cannae wait tae see him, but it's no' lucky afore the weddin'."

The two families enjoyed sharing stories and renewing their relationship and Mary was happy that others from the various camps had accepted and welcomed their arrival. Mary felt a deep sense of contentment, which was something that she had not anticipated.

"Are ye still tellin fortunes Mary?" asked Coralina.

"Aye, an' Ah saw this in the Tarot cards but Ah didnae realise it was you comin' back. Ye could have knocked me o'er wi' a feather, it was such a shock tae see yer face in the crowd." They both laughed and shared their memories of that first moment.

Chapter 45

Mary felt sure that tonight, the night before her beloved Rosa's wedding, she would sleep well, and it would be a deep contented sleep, but that was not to be. The temptation to look at the Tarot was just too great. John was sound asleep, the effect of too many beers; Rosa was exhausted from all the excitement and travel, and she was sleeping soundly too. Mary slipped out of her bed and rummaged in her bag for her Tarot Cards. She threw a shawl over her shoulders, picked up a blanket to sit on, and slipped out of the wagon. She looked around to see if anyone was about, but all was quiet.

She slipped away from all the other wagons and sat quietly under a tree. She settled herself on the grass sitting on the blanket that she had taken with her. It was a cool still night and the moon was full as she opened the satin cloth and placed it on the blanket in front of her. She held her Tarot cards in her hands and thought of the wedding. She fanned the cards in a semi circle, face down on the satin cloth, paused, and then choose one, the six Cups, she smiled knowing exactly what that meant. She sat for a little while thinking about the meeting with her sister and her family and then she choose another card. This time it was the two Cups and once again, she smiled because this was Rosa and Eddie making their promise to each other.

She wondered why she was torturing herself because each time she drew a card her stomach churned with fear, the fear that she might see something that would frighten or worry her. She just wanted to know that everything would be all right in Rosa's future, but Tarot never speaks to please, Tarot shows everything that can happen, good or bad, and it's up to the individual to make the best of changing circumstances and events. Tarot can tell you that something is wrong, but it seldom actually tells you exactly how this will occur, and often, there is nothing that you can do to change things.

She turned another card and it was The Wheel again. She was drawing the same cards, but that was no surprise either because she understood that her situation was the same as it had been the last time she looked, but she wanted to know more, to go further. Bracing herself she took another and this time it was the Eight Branches. She raised her eyebrows and muttered to herself, "That's different, Ah ken whit that is, that's Rosa and Eddie travellin here an' there."

She felt more confident now and took another card, and this time she was thrilled because the card she turned over was the Empress, the young pregnant woman. "A bairn!" she exclaimed to herself as she placed her hands over her heart, this was her dearest wish for Rosa because she knew that Rosa wanted to be a mother. There was no stopping her now, and she took another card and this time she wasn't so pleased. She had drawn the Nine Swords and she knew that this was not a good card, but as is the way when faced with a card that you don't like you are almost compelled to draw another, she did. It was the Ten Swords and her heart was racing.

Her heart was conflicting with her common sense and she had to take another. Things did not get any better for the next card that she turned over was the Three Swords a red heart pierced by three Swords. This was bad, and she had to keep going, but when she turned the next card over, she wished that she had stayed in bed, and remained ignorant, for she had drawn The Tower. She was shaking now, and all her worst fears were materialising before her eyes. She had to choose another, hoping that the next card would assure her that all would be well. She had to bite her knuckles to keep from screaming because the card that she drew meant a funeral. She did not know whose funeral it would be, but she was sure that what she had seen would come to pass, and it would affect her family.

She cried for a long time, but eventually she had to go back to her wagon before anyone woke up. She put the cards away and vowed that she would never read for herself again and lay down on the bed beside John. He stirred and whispered, "Where have ye been?"

"The dunny," she lied.

She stayed awake and got up first thing to wake Rosa, and to help her to get ready for her special day. She managed to carry herself and hide her fears, but her emotions spilled over and anyone who saw her tears assumed they were just the tears of the mother of the bride, dreading her only child leaving to begin a new life. Rosa was ready and looked beautiful in her dress with the long veil cascading down her back.

"Ah'll see ye at the top o' the hill Rosa, yer Da will bring ye up. There's a fair crowd gathered tae wish ye well hinny." She took Rosa in her arms and held her tight, tears streaming down her face, and then she turned, her heart breaking, and left the wagon.

"Ah'm ready Da," said Rosa. She was glowing as all brides are. John looked at his daughter and said, "Yer as beautiful as yer Ma was on her weddin' day. Ah'm right proud o' ye an' Ah'm happy for ye, but it will break our hearts tae see ye go."

Rosa hugged her father, "Ah love ye Da an' Ah'll miss ye tae, but it'll no' be that long afore we're back at the Green an' then there might be a wee Rosa's tae sit on yer knee."

They both held each other and laughed together at the lovely picture Rosa's words had portrayed, neither of them knowing what would really happen.

Mary, and Coralina with her family beside Eddie's parent's Nellie and Edward stood at the top of the Hill on the edge of The Tinkers Heart. Eddie and Tam were waiting for the bride to appear and the sound of cheering told them that she had started to make her way up the hill.

Mary stood and watched with a deep fear in her heart, pretending that all was well but she knew it wasn't. Someone she loved would die and she knew that this death would be untimely but, she could not tell who it would be, or when it would happen. The crowds parted and she saw John bringing Rosa to the Tinkers Heart, leading her to her destiny, and she cried for what was to come.

The End

Before you go

You have just read the prequel to The Wooden Rose, written on demand by those who read it, loved it, and wanted to know more about the earlier days. If you have not read The Wooden Rose, you can read a preview on the following pages now.

As a writer, I am encouraged when readers email me to tell me how much they have enjoyed my books, and although this is precious to me, it is the reviews that count on Amazon. Please take a moment of your time to review my books on Amazon. Thank you and may you and yours have many blessings

Soraya

The Wooden Rose 1

1889 A Travellers' Camp near Glasgow Green

"Hurry Rosa yer Da wants tae leave in ten minutes."

"Ah'm hurryin Ma, Ah'm goin' as fast as Ah can," said Rosa. She could hardly think straight as she hopped about pulling on her black boots and fastening the laces. She was excited at the thought of seeing Eddie again, tall handsome Eddie with his dark curly hair. She couldn't remember the first time that she saw him, but she had known all her life that he was hers. The last time they had met was at Musselburgh Fair when all the travellers got together to reunite, share good times, meet up with family and friends, and trade with each other.

She was sixteen now, her raven black hair came half way down her back and her green eyes shone under long dark eyelashes. Soon she would marry, and the only boy she would marry was Eddie. Her young heart fluttered when she thought of him. Eddie was so clever with his hands. He was an artist with wood, he didn't just make things, he made beautiful things. He made shelves for his Mam's precious ornaments, and he had carved the shapes himself and painted flowers and ivy down the sides. He made clothes pegs to sell round the doors too, but that was different.

Rosa carried a wooden token in her pocket. When no one was watching, she would take the token out of her pocket, look at it, and think of Eddie. Her Eddie had made it for her when he was fourteen and she was only ten. He had carved a lovely rose on the surface of it, and each time she looked at it or held it in her pocket, she thought of her Eddie. It was just a simple piece of wood, flat, about two inches across and half an inch thick, but she could feel the love in it. She was never without it and had never shown it to anyone. It was something special to her and Eddie.

"Hurry up lass," her father called as he hitched the horses to the front of the wagon.

"Stop yer day dreamin' and get up on the wagon."

She loved her Father; he was a big strong man with black curly hair, arms like tree trunks and hands like shovels. They were taking horses he had bred and trained to trade at the fair.

They were leaving Glasgow today, and it would be two or three days before they would reach Musselburgh. Soon they would meet up with friends and family. There would be horseracing and reunions. The young girls would be posing and showing off new dresses that their mothers or grannies had sewn for them, and young men, boys really, would be strutting and acting manly. Everything had to be perfect in this very proud culture and each family would vie to be and have the best; everyone went to Musselburgh Fair, it was traditional.

Mary's Mother had taught her how to scrub, clean, stack, and stow everything that they needed in, on, and around the big wagon. Pots and pans hung from the sides of the wagon and sang a merry note as they travelled. Everything was spic and span, for they were fussy about cleanliness.

Each night after a long day in the wagon, John would stop in the same place that his family had done for generations before him. There were trees to shelter the tent that they would put down to sleep in, because the wagon would be full of things that they needed when they were travelling and things that they could sell or swop. There was lush grass for the horses to graze on, and a running stream nearby for fresh water.

As soon as the wagon stopped, Mary and Rosa would jump down and begin to unpack the things they would need. They always carried wood to start the fire and Rosa would set that out. Mary would gather the slats from where they were stored under the wagon and she would use these to build a floor for their tent. They often erected their big tent if they were staying somewhere for a week or more, but when they were travelling, the smaller tent was fine for their needs.

With the fire started, Rosa helped her mother while John roped off an area and untied the trading horses from the wagon before turning them loose in the secured space. The lead horses were unhitched and turned loose with the others.

Their two terriers ran around excited to be free, but their big lurcher Suzie was tethered safely, with just enough rope to wander a short distance, otherwise she would have been off exploring and hunting for game. Mary set up the chitty prop, a three legged cast iron pyramid shape with a large hook for holding a pot over a fire, as Rosa fetched the water. Fire lit, kettle on to boil water for tea, and animals tended to, they could now sit and rest a while under the stars.

This is how they travelled; always following familiar routes and stopping at familiar places, each place would hold memories of previous times and previous journeys. Each morning they would rise early, feed the animals, and stow all their belongings back in and around the wagon and continue on their journey.

As they neared Musselburgh, they would catch sight of others travelling to the fair and there was a stir of excitement in the air. Finally, they arrived and lined up in a queue to enter the grassy field. They waved and called to other families arriving or queuing. They could see the Morrison's, the Wilson's, and the Boswell's and there were others approaching that they would know, and some of their own family, their second cousins, the Stewarts, would be there too.

Rosa could hardly contain herself.

"Mind yer ane business Rosa and dinnae let yer Da catch you ey'in up these boys," her mother whispered.

Rosa was horrified and embarrassed "I'm no' ey'in up boys, Ah was jist lookin' for…"

"I know who yer lookin for," replied her mother. "It's that Eddie McGuigan. A guid boy mind ye, but dinnae show yer keen."

Rosa blushed and her ears were burning with embarrassment.

"I like him Ma, he asked me to remember him last year."

"Wheesht, here's yer Da!"

The Wooden Rose 2

It was a hard life being a traveller, but it was a good life and a life that they loved. Mary, Rosa's mother, was a good-looking woman of average height and build, but it was her dark hair and eyes and her self-confidence that made her stand out. She always knew what to do and got on with doing it. There was nothing shy or retiring about Mary, and that was what her husband Johnny loved most about her.

Mary always got what she wanted, and in her younger days, she had had a nasty mean streak about her, but that was before she and John got together. She was more understanding and tolerant as an adult than she had ever been. He was known everywhere for his knowledge and skill with the horses, and it was probably that same skill that he used on Mary, settling her when she was about to fly off in a tantrum, or calming her when she was agitated.

Mary had two loves in her life; Rosa, her darling daughter and John, her big strong husband who in spite of his outward stern appearance, had a soft kindly heart and would do anything to help another. John didn't take any nonsense from anyone though, and could drive a hard bargain making sure that he got the best of any deal.

The sun was shining as John was unhitching his horses from the wagon while Mary and Rosa began to fetch the makings for their tent. They unloaded slats of wood from underneath the wagon for the big tent and with the help of nearby children; they began to put it together.

The wooden shapes for the floor went down first to establish the hexagon shape, leaving an uncovered space in the centre for the stove that they carried with them. Other children would dash in to help, and each would hold a length of wood while Mary and Rosa secured poles to the tops, holding the frame together and maintaining the shape.

There was lots of laughing and teasing as the children supported the frame, then Rosa and Mary, standing on either side of the frame began to throw and catch a big tarpaulin cover up and over. The tarpaulin had cords attached at various points to make the job of pulling the cover over easier.

Often they collapsed on the ground laughing and rubbing their aching arms from the effort of the task. Coloured cloths were fetched from the wagon and draped on the inside walls, and rugs were laid on the boards.

Finally, the stove was set up in the middle of the floor, and a long pipe attached to fit directly under the smoke hole at the top of the tent. The stove would keep them warm at night and with a kettle at the ready, there was always a cuppa for anyone who called in.

Outside, Mary set up the chitty prop, and young Rosa fetched the wood to start the fire. Before long, a large cast iron pot of soup or stew would be hanging from the chitty prop. Food was always cooked outside, keeping the tent free from smells and spills. There was always plenty to share among friends and family members.

The muscles in Eddie's arms bulged below the rolled up sleeves of his red and black checked shirt as he set up at the fair though he was oblivious to the admiring glances from some of the young girls. Thick dark hair framed his handsome face tanned with the summer sun. All he could think about was seeing his Rosa.

Eddie was a hard worker and talented too, he just put his head down and got on with things, and when he was working with wood, his mind would drift off into his plans for the future, the future he saw with Rosa. He knew that he was going to marry Rosa and that they would make a family together.

He could see it in his mind's eye as though it had already happened. A big family, boys and girls; the girls would help their Mam and marry well and the boys, well they would work with him. He would teach them how to look at a windfall tree trunk that others would pass by, and he would show them how to read the wood and see what things they could make from it. He would teach his sons how to create beautiful pieces of work that the wealthy would have on show in their fancy homes.

He was twenty now and had been learning to hone his gift for carpentry since he was a child, starting off just whittling bits of wood into little ornaments, making clothes pegs and selling them door to door. Eddie progressed to making three-legged stools and by the time he was in his teens, he was making special pieces; wooden spoons for stirring the pot, bowls, beautifully turned, carved and polished, containers with lids for sugar and tea, children's pull along toys, garden furniture, and wooden ornaments that the wealthy were happy to purchase. He had made good money and saved every penny he could. He was going to speak to Rosa's Father when he saw him next. He knew he could give her a good life with the money he had put by and his plans for the future.

Rosa was helping her mother to set up their camp when out of the corner of her eye she saw Eddie approaching. She glanced quickly at her mother as her cheeks began to glow bright red.

"Ma," she whispered.

"I see him."

Rosa kept her eyes downcast as Eddie approached, and not once did Eddie look in her direction.

"Excuse me, Aunty Mary," he said, as was the custom in his culture, "Could Ah speak tae Uncle John?"

"Ye've never had a problem speakin' tae him before Eddie, dae ye think ye might have wan the noo."

Eddie shuffled his feet showing his discomfort, but he could see that Mary was teasing him. Just at that moment, Uncle John appeared back from chatting to other family members who had just arrived.

"Eddie," he said, looking at Eddie sternly under heavy dark bushy eyebrows. Eddie's stomach might have been churning, but that was no comparison to what John was feeling. He knew in his soul what was coming, but he wasn't ready to let the apple of his eye, his little Rosa, go that easily.

"Uncle John, a word."

"Well, spit it out and Ah'm warnin' ye, Ah'm nae in the best o moods,"

Eddie bristled at John's sharp tone. "Ah could come back an' see ye."

"Jist git on wi' it lad, Ah've things tae dae."

Eddie drew himself up to his full height, stuck out his chin and his chest, looked his uncle in the eye, and said, "It's an important thing Ah wish tae speak tae ye about, but if ye huvnae time tae be civil Ah'll come back."

"Jist haud yer horses' lad, ye got me on the wrong foot. Ah feel Ah know whit ye want to speak tae me about an it's churnin' in ma' stomach. Say yer piece."

John stepped closer to Eddie to put his arm over his shoulder. Surprised by the fact that Eddie was taller than he thought, he wondered why he hadn't noticed, he was dealing with a full-grown man now, but in his mind and heart, to John, Eddie was still a lad. He did what any other proud man would do to avoid his embarrassment, and stuck his hands in his pockets.

"Let's take a walk," he said to the young man.

They walked in silence away from the hustle and bustle of everyone chatting and setting up for the fair. Both men were a generation apart, but both with the same person in mind. Finally, Eddie stopped, looked his uncle in the eye as he looked back at him, took a deep breath, and said, "Ah've loved yer lass since Ah was wee, an' she was just a babe. Ah've watched her grow and become the beautiful lass like the flower ye named her for. The past four years Ah've worked and saved and every penny is for Rosa's future."

His uncle fixed his gaze on him, just stared at him silently saying nothing while his mind went into overdrive.

The words poured out of Eddie like a desperate plea. "Ah'm askin' ye for her hand man," he almost shouted.

John stared at him, the fear becoming a reality, the pain of that reality written on his face.

"Same time, same place, next year, if ye still feel the same ye can ask her yirsel, an' if she agrees ye can marry on the first day of May at the Tinkers Heart."

Eddie's face lit up, he punched the air and did a dance right there in front of John.

"She'll say aye, I know it."

Eddie ran off back to his pitch and as John walked back to his wagon he watched Rosa helping her mother.

"Ah've jist seen that young Eddie," he said to no one in particular, but really so that Rosa could hear. "Turned into a fine man," he said, and climbed into his wagon where he poured himself a whisky, sat down and stared at the wall in front of him, seeing nothing but the memories of his daughter's birth and early years. Thinking of her blossoming into a beautiful woman, he wondered how he would feel to let her go, to start her own life. When Mary came in his face was wet with tears, she sat beside him and reached over, placed her hand in his and gave it a comforting squeeze. No words were necessary between them for she understood how he felt.

The Wooden Rose 3

The atmosphere at the Musselburgh Fair was electric and exciting. Friends and families merged and mingled, lurchers and terriers barked, children played, and the men did what men do. They traded horses, ponies, and dogs, showed their Persian rugs, tin pots and other crafts and looked on proudly at their sons and daughters. They exchanged wares and ideas on how to make a living, places to go to sell their wares, and places to avoid.

The men were a sight to see, all wearing jackets, flat caps, and often waistcoats below. Shirts tucked into dark trousers were clean and white with no collars, but a colourful patterned scarf at the neck. They all stood in a group making loud exchanges as they performed the almost religious ceremony of trading and bargaining. With each offer or counter offer, the men would slap hands, but even that had a specific format. A spit on the palm and a full-handed slap was a deal, but if only fingertips slapped then the bargaining would continue. The seller held his hand out asking, and the buyer would state his offer and slap. The men had idiosyncrasies that would give each other clues to what they were thinking. Some would touch their caps between slaps. Some would turn and pretend to be walking away. Others would complain loudly and throw accusations, but there was always a bargain sealed.

A horse buyer would gradually make his way around so that he could stand directly in front of the horse seller and pretend to be mildly interested. He might stroke the horse, have a look at its teeth, pick up a leg, and feel its joints. The seller would know by this that a sale was imminent and the bargaining would begin.

"Guid enough horse." (Slap)

"What'll ye offer?" (Slap)

"Forty an' not a penny more." (Slap)

"Ah yer jokin' man; Sixty an' not a penny less." (Slap)

"Sixty? Yer a robber Ah'll give forty-five." (Slap)

"Fifty an' ye have a deal."

A spit on the palm and a hand held out, a spit on the palm and a full-handed slap and the deal done.

"Now gimmie a penny back for luck," the buyer would say, and as was the custom, the seller would give the buyer a coin or two and the bargain was sealed.

Young men would stand by and watch the exchanges learning the craft, and then they would discuss among themselves the skills or failings that they had witnessed.

"Aye, he couldha got cheaper," or "He couldha got more if he hung oot a bit."

They in their way would take on board lessons that they had learned, that they would use themselves when their time came. Overloaded with testosterone, they rode their horses bareback, raced each other, and performed tricks to impress the girls. The girls giggled and looked coy and pretended to be unimpressed by the boys.

In the middle of all this, the women gossiped and bragged about their children while they skinned hares for the pot. Some chopped vegetables and fetched split peas and lentils that had been soaked overnight. Dumplings and potatoes added to the stew ensured that there was plenty of filling food all.

Everyone gathered around the campfires and shared the food that had been prepared earlier in the day, and then out would come the pipes and the tobacco for a relaxing smoke. Some of the old grannies would smoke a clay pipe and ponder while they remembered and shared stories about their own younger days.

Those that could play a tune would fetch a musical instrument, fiddles would be fine-tuned, flutes prepared, and box accordions stretched and squeezed. Some would have the traditional Celtic drum the bodhran, and others would be happy with a tambourine or a set of spoons. Others still, with no instrument, would sit open legged on a wooden box and tap a rhythm on the box to accompany the music.

The women and girls would dance and twirl on boards laid out for the purpose; boxes were set out around the space for others to sit on and participate, playing an instrument, or singing, or just enjoying the spectacle. The atmosphere was warm, friendly and exciting, the smell of wood smoke from the fire scented the air, and the night was clear and bright under the full of the moon.

Eddie and Rosa sat side by side quietly chatting. She felt pretty in her new dress, with its full drindle skirt that she had helped her mother to sew. With her head down, she studied the bright blues and reds of the fabric as she wondered what to say to Eddie. They both felt different now that Eddie had declared his intentions. He told Rosa what her father had said. For now, they could sit together or hold hands, perhaps even sneak a kiss if no one was watching, but all eyes would be on them now for it's the traveller's way to be chaste before marriage.

After the fair, the only way that they could communicate would be by messages passed by word of mouth, or for those that could read and write, and at that time, there were only a few with this skill, a note. It would be twenty years before a public telephone appeared, but there were so many of their kind that it was always possible to pass a message from one to another by those who were moving from place to place.

"Ah'm sixteen now, next August when we come to the fair next year Ah'll be seventeen. If ma Da says we can marry on the first of May Ah'll be nearly eighteen an' you'll be nearly twenty-two. It all seems so far away," she said as she looked into his dark brown eyes. His dark curly hair fell over his brow and curled over his collar at the back. They were so entranced with each other that at first they were unaware of the chant.

"Rosa, Rosa, Rosa, give us a dance."

She giggled and got up and moved to the centre of the circle and gave an exaggerated bow. Everyone knew Rosa loved to dance, and had she not been so engrossed in conversation with Eddie, she would have been the first to start the dancing.

The fiddle stuck up, the flutes joined, and the circle of folk began to clap in time to the music. The bodhran beat out its rhythm and Rosa threw her head back with a laugh. She began to dance a jig, her feet matching the rhythm on the boards. She held her skirts up a tiny bit and her black laced boots were visible below them. Round and round the circle she danced, skipping and twirling, the sound of her heels joining the beat of the music, her dark hair flying behind her and then she began to pull other girls into the circle where they joined in the fun of the dance. She was so happy that she wished she was married to Eddie now, and that this could be the beginning of their life together.

As the night ended, a singing voice filled the air and Rosa knew that it was her Father. He was singing the song that his Father used to sing to his Mother.

Johnny was born in a mansion doon in the county o' Clare

Rosie was born by a roadside somewhere in County Kildare

Destiny brought them together on the road to Killorglan

One day in her bright tasty shawl, she was singing

And she stole his young heart away

For she sang...

Meet me tonight by the campfire

Come with me over the hill.

Let us be married tomorrow

Please let me whisper 'I will'

What if the neighbours are talkin'

Who cares if yer friends stop and stare

Ye'll be proud to be married to Rosie,

Who was reared on the roads of Kildare.

Think of the parents who reared ye

Think of the family name

How can ye marry a Gypsy?

Oh whit a terrible shame

Parents and friends stop yer pleading

Don't worry aboot my affair

For Ah've fallen in love wi' a Gypsy

Who was reared on the roads of Kildare?

Johnny went down from his mansion

Just as the sun had gone doon

Turning his back on his kinfolk

Likewise, his dear native toon

Facing the roads of old Ireland

Wi' a Gypsy he loved so sincere

When he came to the light of the campfire

These are the words he did hear

Meet me tonight by the campfire

Come wi' me over the hill.

Let us be married tomorrow

Please let me whisper 'I will'

What if the neighbours are talkin?

Who cares if yer friends stop and stare

Ye'll be proud to be married to Rosie,

Who was reared on the roads of Kildare.

DEDICATION ACKNOWLEDGMENTS

With thanks to my readers whose kind words, following the publication of my first novel The Wooden Rose, have encouragement to keep writing novels.

With thanks to my husband Martin, who patiently edits my dyslexic mistakes, repeatedly. Thanks go to everyone who reads this book and help me to follow my dreams as a writer

About the Author

Soraya began her professional writing career as the resident astrologer for The Sunday Post newspaper. In 2001 Soraya was invited to write her first reference book **'Book of Spells'** which continues to be a best seller and since then she has gone on to write other titles in this genre.

As a Reiki Master Teacher Soraya devoted much of her time to developing Reiki Teaching manuals that maintain traditional methods yet provide best practice for expected educational standards and her courses were credit rated to graduate level by The Scottish Qualifications Authority (SQA). Soraya has published The Reiki Training Manual to share her experience and although she has now retired from teaching Reiki, Master Teachers trained by her are still teaching Soraya's methods.

Her psychic skills are apparent in one of her latest books 'Psychic Guidance'. This was inspired because readers of her Book of Runes commented that when they had a problem all they had to do was open her Rune book and they would find their answer. With this in mind, Soraya put Psychic Guidance together to help others in times of need. All they have to do is think of their question and open the book at a random page to find their guidance.

Soraya's secret ambition has always been to write novels but she always felt too busy to devote any time to doing what she wanted to do most. She achieved that dream with the "The Wooden Rose" and followed this with Before the Rose.

Soraya a White Witch is a bestselling author, Resident Psychic Astrologer & Agony Aunt with My Weekly Magazine,

Also by Soraya

In the Wiccan genre

Book of Spells

Book of Tarot

Book of Runes

Enhance Your Psychic Powers

Psychic Guidance

The Witches Companion

The Kitchen Witch

The Little Book of Spells

The Little Book of Cord and Candle Magick

Education and Training Genre

Reiki Training Manual

Romantic Mystery Fiction

The Wooden Rose, a symbol of love, a mystery unravelled.

Before the Rose, the Gypsy's Curse

Visit Soraya's website and join her mailing list, The Witches Web at www.soraya.co.uk

Printed in Poland
by Amazon Fulfillment
Poland Sp. z o.o., Wrocław

54758785R00159